Summer of Us

a Blue Harbor novel

OLIVIA MILES

Rosewood Press

ALSO BY OLIVIA MILES

Blue Harbor Series
A Place for Us
Second Chance Summer
Because of You
Small Town Christmas
Return to Me
Then Comes Love
Finding Christmas
A New Beginning

Stand-Alone Titles
Summer's End
Meet Me at Sunset
This Christmas

Oyster Bay Series
Feels Like Home
Along Came You
Maybe This Time
This Thing Called Love
Those Summer Nights
Christmas at the Cottage
Still the One
One Fine Day
Had to Be You

Misty Point Series
One Week to the Wedding
The Winter Wedding Plan

Sweeter in the City Series
Sweeter in the Summer
Sweeter Than Sunshine
No Sweeter Love
One Sweet Christmas

Briar Creek Series
Mistletoe on Main Street
A Match Made on Main Street
Hope Springs on Main Street
Love Blooms on Main Street
Christmas Comes to Main Street

Harlequin Special Edition
'Twas the Week Before Christmas
Recipe for Romance

Copyright © 2022 by Megan Leavell
ISBN 979-8-9862624-0-6

All rights reserved. No part of this publication may be reproduced, distributed or transmitted in any form or by any means, without prior written permission.

Publisher's Note: This is a work of fiction. Names, characters, places, and incidents are a product of the author's imagination. Locales and public names are sometimes used for atmospheric purposes. Any resemblance to actual people, living or dead, or to businesses, companies, events, institutions, or locales is completely coincidental.

Summer of Us

1

It was not lost on Heidi Clark that her sisters, cousins, and most of her friends (okay, make that all of her friends) had moved out of their parents' houses when they were eighteen, maybe dropping back in for a bit after college, but certainly not beyond that. That they had apartments or homes or businesses or even families of their own by now. And that she didn't have any of that—yet.

Heidi had been in and out of her parents' house for years, sometimes staying for a month, or, like recently, sometimes several months. But that was then and this was now. She made a silent promise to herself as she sealed the last box with tape that this time, she was moving out of her childhood home for good. She'd be thirty years old in a matter of weeks. There was no going back this time.

Technically, she'd been living in the carriage house a few hundred yards from the cozy Victorian where she'd grown up, with her own door and even her own mailbox, but her parents had been forgiving on rent, her mother still offered to do her laundry whenever she had a load to put in, and she wasn't shy about letting herself in with her key, sometimes making Heidi's bed in the process. There was always a fridge full of food in the kitchen of the main house, and often a hot meal, too. Sometimes one that included dessert. And who was Heidi to turn down a freshly

baked pie with a scoop of ice cream after a long day? Who would want to give that all up? It was a pretty sweet deal, perhaps, but it was also an aching reminder that Heidi didn't have her life together while her sisters and cousins did.

Today, all of that was going to change.

"Are you sure that you don't need any help moving all your things over?" Bella, Heidi's middle sister, should probably be at the bookstore she owned and operated right now, but she'd taken a long lunch break to offer her support.

"You've done enough," Heidi said, giving her a reassuring smile. And it was true. Bella had given her a second chance at the store, and this time around, it had worked out. She'd followed Bella's system and rules, even if she didn't agree with them, though this time, instead of just doing things the way she thought best, she suggested new ideas instead—ones that, to her surprise, Bella had taken into consideration and even put into effect. Now the bookstore was thriving, Heidi had something meaningful to show on her resume, and she had a steady paycheck, too. Not much considering she was only needed part-time in the store, but enough to lease the two-bedroom cottage within walking distance to town, especially when she combined it with everything she'd stashed away while not exactly paying rent on the current space, much as she tried to offer.

She almost laughed as she sealed the last of the boxes. And her family didn't think she was responsible? She could have blown that cash on clothes, drinks, or even weekend trips, but instead, she'd stowed it away, preparing for this day. The day when she finally showed her sisters and her parents and her cousins and all the other naysayers in town who thought of her as something less than responsible that she was an adult.

An almost thirty-year-old adult. Really, she probably shouldn't have to prove anything, but she did. And this new lease was the start.

"The cottage is furnished, so all I have to worry about are my clothes and a few other things I've collected over the years." That wasn't saying much. She had her pillow, her bedding, towels, and some sentimental objects like framed photos and random pieces of costume jewelry along with the clothes that she would now be washing herself. "I'll borrow Mom's car and then take my bike over after the last trip."

Would it be nice to eventually have a car? Sure. But that was one area where she didn't feel like it was a reflection of her place in life. Here in Blue Harbor, you could walk or bike to most places. It was the charm of their small town, especially this time of year when the sun was bright and warm and the streets were full of tourists and locals alike, enjoying the contrast of the cool lake breeze and the hot, summer afternoons.

"With all the noise from their renovations, you must be looking forward to some peace and quiet." Bella's eyes widened when, as if on cue, the sound of a drill blasted through the open window.

Heidi crossed the room to close it. She wouldn't bother pointing out that the construction had played a factor in

her deciding it was time to get a place of her own. What had started out as a "refresh" was turning into a full rehab of their parents' home, with more trucks crowding the gravel driveway each day, and more crews starting work earlier and earlier each morning.

When she'd had a wonderful dream about her high school crush (never mind that he was now married and living six doors down the street or that even when she was fifteen and she'd begged her sisters to do a drive-by of his house while she worked up the courage to ask him to the Sadie Hawkins' dance, he had no interest in her either) interrupted by Sonny, the lead contractor with a booming voice that could be heard over the rattle of a window-box air-conditioning unit at ten minutes before seven on Saturday—a Saturday!—she'd officially received the kick she needed. Until then she'd been thinking (because contrary to most people's assumptions about her, she did plan some things) that she'd wait until the end of the year, after the holidays, to give herself more time to save up money and make sure that her work experience at the bookstore wasn't a fleeting fluke. But unless she wanted more men in her dreams to start calling out the names of tools, change was needed.

And at the rate her love life was going, the only men in her life existed in her sleep.

"I can't believe you managed to find a place at this time of year. Usually, all the rentals are gone well before summer."

"Just came on the market." Heidi shrugged. The Tinleys had lived in Blue Harbor all their lives, but with their children spread out across the country, they wanted to be closer to family. When their daughter announced she was pregnant with twins two weeks ago, they upped and moved, deciding there was no time like the present. "I just hope they don't miss Blue Harbor too much and want to move back for part of the year."

"Summer in Blue Harbor is pretty hard to beat," Bella agreed.

Heidi could already see her plans falling apart before they'd even come to fruition. She could envision herself schlepping her boxes back to this very carriage house, only this time she'd be sharing the space with her parents, who would be residing in it until their renovations were complete.

In other words, not an option.

She chewed a nail nervously and then dropped her hand. Nail-biting was all in the past. And today was supposed to be the first day of her future!

"They decided not to sell, which means they aren't ready to let go just yet."

"They're probably keeping it to pass down to their children," Bella assured her. "They're probably hoping that someday they'll be summer people."

"Well, not this summer." And it wasn't like the cottage would be her forever home. But she'd love to make something last at least a year, or more. A loud crash from outside made Heidi wince. "The timing is perfect. Mom and Dad can move in here until the renovations are finished, and I can walk to work."

"About that…" Bella started, but Heidi held up a hand.

"Let's not talk about my long-term career plans today," she warned. She was scheduled to meet the real estate agent at the cottage to collect the key in less than an hour, and again, Bella should really get back to the shop soon. "Besides, don't you have a dog to walk?"

Bella gave a fond smile as she did anytime her puppy was mentioned. "Craig took him to the park."

Now it was Heidi's turn to smile. Recently, her sister's life had changed for the better. She not only had sweet little George in her life but a new boyfriend, too. It was proof that the rest of your life could start today if you were open to change. And Heidi was.

"Well, I'm sure that they'll be expecting you soon. Besides, as you said, it's a busy time of the year in Blue Harbor. And if no one's manning the shop—"

Once a talk about her career would have been along the lines of being encouraged to find a job, any job, and stick with it. Now that she'd discovered that her endless ideas and big-picture mentality were a benefit to Bella's bookstore, her sister, who couldn't afford to employ her full time, was forever hinting that she should think about taking her services to other businesses in town.

It was a whole new set of stress, and it was just as overwhelming. As if she didn't have enough going on at the moment.

Bella held up a hand, laughing. "Okay, now's not the time, but when you're ready, you know I'm more than happy to write you a letter of recommendation."

Heidi felt her chest swell with gratitude. Her sister believed in her, which was something she probably wouldn't have been able to say just a few months ago, when she was yet again unemployed, or "between opportunities" as she liked to say. She was on the right path.

"Thanks, Bella. For everything. I mean it." She grinned and raised her arms to stretch her back. "Hey, why don't you let me treat you to dinner at my new place once I'm settled? I'll actually have my own kitchen."

Technically, it wasn't the first time, but the short-term apartments she'd lived in before had kitchens the size of closets that she often shared with a roommate or two.

Bella looked skeptical. "I can bring takeout."

There it was again. The hidden belief that Heidi didn't totally have her life together, not like her sisters or cousins. That she lived off cereal and coffee and granola bars or her mother's home cooking, which, okay, wasn't a huge stretch but a little insulting, nonetheless.

"I'll cook," she said firmly. And she'd be sure to make it the most delicious meal she'd ever cooked.

Even if it admittedly might be one of the first.

*

Ryan Harrison looked up from the computer screen and rubbed his eyes. It had been over a year since he'd moved back to his Michigan hometown and taken over the family pub, and despite the changes he'd implemented, the numbers still weren't heading in the direction he'd hoped. At least not fast enough for his liking.

He could spend another day, sitting here, going over receipts and menus and pacing the floor trying to figure things out, or he could worry about his personal life for a few hours instead.

The sound of the movers on the stairs over his head was his answer.

"All packed up," one said, appearing in the office doorway. He mopped the sweat from his brow with a cloth before shoving it in his back pocket.

Ryan nodded. He'd known this day was coming. He'd planned for it like he did everything. The space above the pub where he'd lived for the better part of the past year would soon house the storage and administrative space, leaving additional space on the main floor for a much-needed expansion of the dining room—and some better ventilation in the process. It was progress. Meant to drive traffic and increase revenue.

But it was also change. And in this case, it was a goodbye. This had been his father's office, the very desk where he'd sat day after day, where Ryan's brother Kyle had also sat when he'd taken over the place seven years ago. And for the past year, it had been Ryan's. Unexpected for the entire family, most of all for him. But the legacy had become a privilege. And even though the desk and chair and everything else housed in this cramped space would simply be moved upstairs, it would be different. A new era. A reminder that he'd made a commitment. That good or bad, he had to see this pub through.

He could only hope that there were more good days ahead. He owed his brother that much, for carrying the weight of it on his own for so long. And he owed it to his mother, who believed in him.

But most of all, he owed it to his father, even if he wasn't here anymore. Perhaps especially because he wasn't here anymore.

"I'll meet you over at the cottage," Ryan told the movers, who had packed up his few furnishings and boxes to cart over to his new residence. It wasn't far, walking distance, really, but he decided to drive so he could make the most use of his day. He didn't have time to stroll down Main Street, didn't even have time to house hunt. That was all part of the appeal of the cottage: the location was prime, the space was furnished, and Rex Tinley had been a regular at the pub and a friend of his father's. It was a win-win. The Tinleys could settle into their new condo near their grandkids with peace of mind that their property was being taken care of, and eventually, they could pass down the investment to their children, who rarely visited these parts anymore, Rex had said with a shake of his head, stirring up Ryan's own guilt.

He hadn't visited much either. Certainly not enough. And moving back had never been in the plans. All proof that anything was possible, he supposed.

For now, he was just happy to have a place of his own, somewhere to put down roots in the town he'd decided to call home for the long haul. Unless the pub had to shutter its doors for good.

Pushing back his chair, he shook off that thought. He was moving in the right direction. Taking risks, making changes. Tomorrow the construction crew would start their work.

Ryan picked up the keys and paused in the doorway, taking one good look around the room while one of the movers waited in the hallway, ready to start lifting file cabinets and carrying everything upstairs.

With a lump in his throat, he turned and walked out the door. He'd never been one to shy away from change, and today was no different, he told himself firmly.

It was the last hurdle in his relaunching of the pub.

Oh, who was he kidding? It was the pub's last hope.

*

Lanie Thompson was waiting on the front stoop when Heidi stepped out of the car. Excitement rolled through her stomach as she walked up the flagstone path toward the blue-painted front door of what was officially her new home. Its clapboard siding was painted white and a stark contrast to the thick green grass and flowering shrubs that hugged the base of the front windows.

When she'd toured it two weeks ago, she'd fallen in love with the sunny kitchen, even if she didn't cook much—yet. The yard was bursting with flowers both front and back, and the rooms were cozy and well furnished, with slipcovered sofas and chairs and threadbare rugs in faded shades of blue and green. The cottage was small, with a living room that doubled as a dining room off the kitchen, and two small bedrooms that shared a bathroom. There wouldn't be much to do other than move in, unpack a few boxes to give it a personal touch, and pour a glass of wine while she let it all soak in.

Lanie jangled the keys for her and then retrieved a bottle of champagne from her oversized tote. "A housewarming gift."

Housewarming. It was just a rental, but it was Heidi's first home. Her other places had all been studio apartments, short-term leases, ones that gave her an easy escape hatch which she often needed. But this place...this was a commitment. One she hoped she could live up to. One that was a long-term promise not only to the landlords but also to herself that she could do this.

"Want to come in and pop it open?" Heidi noticed the bottle was already chilled, but then Lanie was thoughtful that way. She paid attention to the details, which was probably why she was so successful. The county's number one real estate agent two years in a row, and she was only a handful of years older than Heidi.

She was, like so many of the women in town, an inspiration.

"I'll have to take a rain check," Lanie said with a shake of her head. "I have a closing in thirty minutes across town."

"It's that time of year," Heidi said, stepping back to take in the small front porch. She'd save up and put a chair in the corner, maybe some potted plants, too. She could already imagine sipping coffee while she watched Main Street come alive each morning.

"There's no better place to sell property than Blue Harbor," Lanie agreed. "Of course, being a buyer is a different story. There aren't enough of these charming places to go around, especially homes with waterfront views. By the way, if your parents are ever willing to sell, I probably have three buyers already lined up with a cash offer."

"My parents are actually renovating," Heidi told her. "I don't think they have any plans to leave Blue Harbor anytime soon." And she was glad for it. Once, it would have

been because she needed them, depended on them to do little things like, oh, house and feed her, sometimes clothe her, but since she'd started insisting on paying rent (or a portion of it, whatever they would accept) for the carriage house, and buying her own food (at least on the nights that a hot lasagna or cool lemon meringue pie weren't already on the table), she'd noticed a shift in their relationship, and one for the better. She wasn't ready to have them flee for warm weather and tropical breezes just yet.

Lanie raised an eyebrow. "A renovation will only increase the value." She grinned, but then spread her arms wide to the cottage. "But today we're talking about your new home. Excited?"

"Excited. Nervous. But mostly excited." Heidi felt her stomach swoop when Lanie set the keys in her palm.

"It's yours for the next twelve months, more if you want to renew. With the Tinleys being so far away, if there are any issues, feel free to contact me directly. I'll be processing all your monthly checks, too."

Heidi sucked in a breath. Just the thought of a monthly check once filled her with anxiety, but now she knew it would all be fine. She'd saved enough to cover the next six months, and between her work at the bookstore and some other ventures she would hopefully get under way soon enough, she wouldn't have a problem if she was responsible.

She almost snorted out loud. Responsible was not a word that most people associated with Heidi Clark. But she was about to show them.

"Thanks for everything, Lanie."

"Of course!" Lanie stepped off the stoop and shielded her eyes from the sun with her hand. "It really is a perfect first home."

It was. And Heidi couldn't wait to get inside.

She waited until Lanie had driven off in her expensive, and very adult-like, sedan before turning and facing the front door. She'd go back for her boxes in a few minutes. First, she wanted to enjoy this moment, experience the rush of sliding the key into the lock, turning the door handle, and stepping into her new home.

And straight into the chest of...

"Ryan Harrison?" She stared up into those deep-set navy-blue eyes, waiting for her heart to resume a normal speed. It wasn't an intruder. Or a burglar. Or even old Mr. Tinley, not quite moved out, which would have been somewhat explainable, though still strange. It was Ryan. Her cousin Brooke's husband's brother and your standard pain in the you know what.

"You scared me!" she accused, but still no apology came. Not that she was surprised. Ryan had always been arrogant, as far back as she could remember. Despite their age difference, their connection to Brooke had meant an overlap in family functions, and in Blue Harbor, there was no escaping anyone. Not even in her own home, it would seem.

He looked equally shocked to see her, and not very pleased. The look was well-practiced. While on paper he hit all the checkboxes for visual appeal (strong jaw, thick head of dark brown hair, deep-set eyes framed by thick brows, and a tall, athletic frame that was accentuated by the white tee shirt) his personality left a lot to be desired.

"What are you doing here?" he demanded. "How did you get in?"

She stared at him, all too aware that her jaw had slackened. "I could ask you the very same thing! This is my house. You nearly gave me a heart attack."

He gave a little smirk. A condescending one, in Heidi's opinion, and she was well-rehearsed with such attitude. "Twenty-five-year-olds don't tend to have heart attacks."

Was he a doctor now? He'd always been smug about his grades, about going away to college and then moving on to a big, corporate career while his brother stayed behind and ran the family pub. But now Ryan was the one running the bar, and he didn't have his facts straight.

"I'm thirty," she said. Almost.

She couldn't tell if that was a flicker of surprise that passed through his gaze or amusement. Oh, who was she kidding? Ryan was anything but lighthearted, and this situation was far from amusing.

"This is my house. I let myself in with my keys." She held them up in the air to prove it.

His eyes narrowed on her. "No, this is my house. As of today."

Heidi blinked rapidly, feeling another dream slip through her hands, and this one bigger, and more impactful. This wasn't her perfume-making business that hadn't panned out or the customized lotions she'd attempted to sell online either. This was her house. This was her fresh start.

"I just watched Lanie drive away. I can assure you that she handled the lease contract. She handed me the keys to the door. For the next twelve months, I live here." Darn it, her voice shook a little.

Ryan stared at her, his expression giving as little away as his lack of response.

"And I just worked out a lease with Mr. Tinley personally. I can assure you that for the next twelve months, I live here. He even asked me to water his plants." Ryan didn't look thrilled with this favor.

It was then that Heidi noticed the stacks of boxes, the ugly painting on the wall that hadn't been here just two weeks ago when she'd toured the home. The smell of coffee coming from the kitchen. Her kitchen. Her sunny, happy, cheerful kitchen. The kitchen where she planned to make a big family meal and present it to all those that still viewed her as a child.

Two things were very clear when she dragged her focus back to Ryan's narrowed gaze.

There was a problem here, and she wasn't sure which was bigger: having someone else in her brand-new home or having that person be the insufferable Ryan Harrison.

2

The old Heidi would have run to her mother, right now, either physically, or through text, or probably both. But this wasn't a problem that her parents or sisters could resolve for her. There wasn't a check to write, or a favor to call in, no. Oh, she almost longed for those simple issues—getting her electricity cut off for not paying the bill in time she could easily fix, but this was big. So big that she had an instinct to walk out the door, back to the comfort of her childhood home, and just shelve that whole "adulting" thing for a while.

Instead, she walked out the door, climbed back into her mother's car that was still filled with her boxes, packed with such care and anticipation that it almost made her weep to look at them, and drove to the real estate office. It took her nearly as long to circle the block for a parking space as it would have to just walk there, but she didn't trust Ryan not to chase her down, and she had to beat him to the finish line on this one, even though he clearly thought he was in the right.

But no, she had a lease. She'd used an actual real estate agent. If anyone could get to the bottom of this, it was Lanie. That was what she was hired to do.

Heidi closed her eyes briefly after parking the car. Yes,

this would all be okay. Because the alternative... She couldn't even think about that right now.

The real estate office was small and the woman at the front desk was the mother of one of Heidi's former classmates. She greeted Heidi with a big smile and proffered a bowl of hard candy.

"Why, Heidi Clark. How are you doing, sweetheart?"

Heidi knew she couldn't take offense to the term of endearment, but right now, she felt all of about six years old, standing here in this professional place of business in her cut-off shorts and ribbed tank top. Her moving clothes. So much for that.

She waved away the candy and cut to the chase. "Is Lanie available? There seems to be a mix-up with my new lease."

"She's in a closing right now, but she should be out within a half hour or so. You can wait?"

Heidi didn't see much choice. She nodded and took a seat near the window. She picked up a magazine that promised thirty summer recipes and flipped to one at random. It would do. Bella would like it. Her sister Natalie, too. And her niece, Zoe, of course.

Yes, she thought, flipping the page. She just had to take a few deep breaths and stay positive. She'd have that dinner party. She would not move back in with her parents today.

"Now tell me, Heidi," Mrs. DiStephano said from across the room, once she'd taken two calls and tapped at her computer for a few minutes. "What are you up to these days?"

Heidi would have loved to announce that today she was

moving into what she hoped would be a long-term living situation, but instead, she managed a tight smile and said, "I've been working at the bookstore."

"Your sister's shop!"

Well, when you put it like that...

Heidi felt her smile wane. Her employment had been a favor, she knew, especially after how disastrous her first time working at Bella's Books had been. One that her mother had put in place, calling on the family card as she tended to do, even though Heidi had made her promise not to, insisting that she would figure things out, that she was almost thirty, that she was capable.

"That's right," she said tightly. She flipped to another page in the magazine, but Mrs. DiStephano unwrapped a butterscotch candy and popped it into her mouth, looking at her intently.

"Weren't you over at that salon in Pine Falls recently?"

Ah yes, the ill-fated job at the salon where she was told that all she would have to do was wash hair. She didn't know about the head massages, or that she didn't know how to do them. When she'd caused one woman to shriek in pain and another to run from the building with sopping wet hair, she'd known her days were numbered.

"It wasn't a fit," she said simply. That was her standard line. Nothing up until now had been a fit, and even working at the bookstore had taken more than one try.

And now Bella wanted to give her the boot. Wanted her to "spread her wings." Just when she was feeling safe.

She cleared her throat and set down the magazine. "How's Bianca?"

That worked like a dream. Mrs. DiStephano beamed. All interest in Heidi's life came to a sudden halt. "Glowing. You know she's expecting, right? Another boy. I think she'll keep trying until she gets that girl!"

Heidi tried not to hide her shock. She and Bianca had been friendly all through school but they'd lost touch when Bianca had gotten married and moved a few towns over to start a family.

Baby number two? And here Heidi had started the day thinking that she was finally catching up with everyone! Instead, she was dangerously close to finding out she was technically homeless.

"And of course, my older daughter just opened that new boutique in Pine Falls," the woman continued.

Heidi swallowed hard, seeing this as a chance to assert herself, knowing that it was an opportunity, and she should seize it, just like Bella had been encouraging her to do. "I'm happy to offer my services if she needs any help spreading the word."

Now Mrs. DiStephano looked at her with a frown. "I thought you were working at your sister's bookstore."

"Yes, but what I've done for her isn't exactly shelving books. I've been helping her…strategize her business." She tried to think of the notes from the pitch she'd been dabbling with in her free time. "I've really helped her grow her revenue in the past month, and market to a broader reach."

Mrs. DiStephano gave a polite smile. After a moment, she said, "You had another job in Pine Falls, didn't you? At that restaurant on the corner near the town hall? Or was it the café down near the water?"

"Both," Heidi said, feeling the familiar dread roil her stomach. Both and then some.

A door clicked in the distance and Mrs. DiStephano was startled. "Looks like the closing ended sooner than expected."

Thank goodness for small favors, Heidi thought, even though she'd had about enough favors for one lifetime.

"Heidi?" Lanie waved off a happy couple and turned to her in confusion. "Is everything okay with the property? I gave you the right set of keys, didn't I? I have such a busy day, I hope I didn't grab the wrong ones."

"The keys worked," Heidi assured her.

Lanie tipped her head toward her office door. "Then what's going on?"

Heidi waited until she was seated in a plush visitor chair, facing Lanie's polished wood executive desk, before speaking. Lanie, wearing her usual pencil skirt and blouse, slid into her oversized swivel chair and smiled at her in expectation.

More aware than ever that Lanie was technically only a few years older than her and somehow had established herself as a highly successful, respectable single woman with a stable career, home, and reputation, Heidi tried to imagine how she would respond to this news—news that seemed could only happen to her, of course.

"Ryan Harrison claims that he is already renting the property."

Lanie looked visibly shocked, saying nothing for a moment. "Ryan Harrison? How did you find this out?"

Heidi chuckled, not happily. "He was inside the house. He'd already made the place his own."

Lanie started rummaging through the files on her desk, finally opening one and reading it over. "But this lease is signed by both parties, effective today. I assure you, the house is yours."

"Ryan said he has a lease too. That he worked it out directly with Mr. Tinley."

Lanie patted her perfect blond bun and pinched her lips thoughtfully. After a breath, she flipped through the lease contract and looked up at Heidi. "Your lease is signed by Mrs. Tinley."

Heidi chewed her lip, hating the way she felt when she looked at Lanie and asked, "So what am I supposed to do now?"

These were the types of questions she hoped to never ask again, not to others, at least.

"I'll get the Tinleys on the phone to sort out this mess but in the meantime, I'd say...talk to Ryan."

Talk to Ryan? The man was impossible. Strangely quiet, which always unsettled her in a person, eerily calm, and the master of a blank expression. He was probably an excellent poker player. She wondered if the man even had teeth. Had anyone ever seen him smile?

"Show him your lease. Give him my card. And convince him that the best thing for everyone involved would be to gracefully exit the premises."

Heidi perked up a little, liking the way that sounded. She nodded and took one of Lanie's thick creamy cards with the embossed lettering in a chic navy font. She'd talk to Ryan, all right. Right now. She'd tell him to exit the premises. Gracefully.

She didn't know what made her feel more grown-up—putting Ryan Harrison in his place, or informing him that he was on her property and that he'd best vacate. Immediately.

*

Ryan stood behind the bar of the pub watching the regular day drinkers nurse their beers with one eye on the television screen. Despite the changes he'd made to the establishment in the year since he'd taken things over from his brother, the crowd hadn't changed as much as he'd hoped, and therefore business hadn't either. Gone were the tired lighting fixtures, the dark shutters, and the dartboards. The pool table had been moved to the back but the noise from it was still steady most nights. The menu had been tweaked but he still couldn't find a way to match the appeal that some of the other places in town had mastered. He was missing something. It was right there; he just had to figure it out. And fast.

The door swung open and Ryan looked up in surprise—first, that it was a woman, because Harrison's still pulled a mostly male clientele, which was frustrating as heck and a problem if the business was going to last much longer. But this wasn't just any woman. This was Heidi Clark. And despite the little smile that curved her mouth as she strode across the scuffed floorboards in long, bare legs and shorts that left little to the imagination, Ryan braced himself for an unpleasant conversation.

"I would have thought you'd still be at the house, unpacking," she said, stopping just short of the bar. A few of the men sized her up, and she nailed them with a scathing look.

Now, Ryan couldn't help but grin.

"I have a job to do," he said simply. "But I take it to mean you admit that the cottage is mine?"

"Quite the opposite." She widened her eyes. They were blue with long lashes. Something he'd never really noticed before. But then, Heidi wasn't someone he'd sought out in the past, and not just because she was...a kid. Heidi was loud and demonstrative and she possessed a kind of energy that made him uneasy.

He couldn't imagine what it would be like to be on Heidi's bad side and he didn't want to find out. She came from a tight family, one that was a force even bigger than her. No doubt the Clarks and the Conways would be banding together as a barricade outside his home by now, and he especially didn't want to tick Brooke off. His brother's wife had been generous to him since he'd moved back, and he'd miss the weekly dinners at their house.

"I can assure you that I have a signed lease," he said, thinking that it might be best for him to just call Lanie Thompson himself. And soon. He'd already put a call in to Rex Tinley, of course, but it had gone straight to voicemail.

"And I do too." She set a folder on the bar top and flipped it over. "Lanie handled everything and I just came from her office. She assured me that this is legal and binding."

Ryan ignored the murmur of interest from the regulars within earshot and nodded down at the papers. "Do you mind?"

"Not at all!" Heidi stepped back from the bar, crossing her arms at her chest. She might be cold, he realized. He kept the air conditioning cranked up, mostly because the clientele preferred it that way. Now he wondered if that might be the problem. Or at least, a factor.

Right now, though, he had other worries. He flipped through the pages of the lease, noting that her rent was at least listed the same as his, the terms of the dates, too. And there, on the last page, was Mrs. Tinley's signature.

Disappointed, he pushed out a breath. "Well, this does look legitimate."

"It is. And you can talk to Lanie if you have any questions." Heidi slapped a business card from the real estate office on the wooden bar top.

Ryan may be running this pub into the ground, but he was no fool when it came to business. He had two degrees and a long career in management. He knew how to read a contract. And he knew enough to make sure what he was signing was on the up and up, too.

"If you follow me to my office, I can show you the lease that Mr. Tinley gave me." He stopped and pinched the space between his eyes. "Actually, I don't have an office at the moment." What he had was a giant mess. The construction crew was scheduled to come tomorrow to tear down the wall between the old office and the current dining room. It would be disruptive, and he'd take a hit for a while.

He slid a glance at the old, bearded men at the corner of the bar. Some patrons wouldn't let the noise deter them from their daily libations, at least.

"What does Lanie suggest we do?"

"She's calling the Tinleys," Heidi said. Ryan's relief was short-lived when Heidi added, "But it will probably come down to us working this out between ourselves. So one of us needs to go, and I can promise you that it won't be me."

"It won't be me either." Ryan, realizing that he'd spoken too loudly, glanced over at the customers and then back to Heidi. "I just cleared out my apartment upstairs. The movers are setting up a new office space there as we speak."

"And I just moved out of my..." Heidi paused to lick her lip. "Apartment. There's a new tenant already moving in. As we speak."

Ryan rubbed a hand over his forehead. There had to be an easy solution. "Don't you have sisters you can move in with? Cousins?"

She leveled him with a narrowed look. "And don't you have a brother?"

He shook his head. Dinner once a week was one thing, but camping out on their couch was another.

"You know that Brooke and Kyle have a small place. Besides, they'll need the extra space for when the baby comes."

Uh-oh. The moment he saw Heidi's eyes pop open, he knew he'd messed up. Kyle and Brooke were waiting to share the news themselves, and the only reason that Ryan knew was because he'd walked in on Kyle building a bassinette in his workshop when he'd dropped by last week a little earlier than usual. He'd been sworn to secrecy, and now he'd gone and told not just someone in town, which was trouble enough, but Brooke's very own cousin.

"They're having a baby?" Heidi swooned with joy. "But I didn't know? When did you find out?"

"Please don't tell anyone," Ryan pleaded in an urgent whisper. But even as he said it, he supposed that his plea would be dismissed. The Clarks and the Conways were ten women strong. Eleven if you counted Candy Conway, who could sniff out gossip from one glance in someone's direction. "Kyle will kill me. Actually, Brooke will kill me. And you know how this town is, you tell one person and then by the end of the day, everyone knows. They plan to make an announcement when the time is right. To everyone."

"My lips are sealed," Heidi said. Sensing his hesitancy, she said. "I mean it."

Did she, though? Because Ryan couldn't remember an event or party they'd both been to where he hadn't seen her and her cousins and sisters whispering and giggling and basically sharing everything.

"Hand to God, Ryan. I won't tell a soul." She set a hand to her own heart, but his relief was short-lived when her mouth curved up. "If you move out of the cottage."

"That's called blackmail," he said frankly. His jaw pulsed with anger. To think he'd almost believed her!

This was typical, classic Heidi Clark. She'd always had a mischievous streak, a gleam in her eyes even when she was still a little girl in pigtails. Always dared someone to jump off the highest rock into the lake, or begged someone to dare her. She was fearless. Maybe even reckless. Whereas he…

Well, there was nothing wrong with being cautious. Especially if recent history had taught him anything.

"That's called a deal," she replied with a shrug.

They were at a standoff. He stared into her eyes—those big, blue, strangely alluring eyes—and then set his jaw.

"I just told you I have nowhere else to go. And I do have a lease. And I don't really believe that you'd do anything to upset your cousin." At least he could only hope so, because the absolute last thing in the world he wanted was to lose his brother's trust when he'd only just regained it.

Her fierce stare lasted about another five seconds before she relaxed her expression. "Oh, fine. You're right. So what do you propose, then? We share the place?"

Ryan sputtered on a laugh. "Share the place? I don't even know you."

"What do you mean? You've known me my entire life."

That was true, technically. But the Heidi Clark he knew was an annoying little girl with a loud laugh, riding her bike through town at breakneck speed, or later, floating from one job to the next, never lasting very long before moving on to the next. He supposed he should be relieved that she hadn't come looking for work at Harrison's yet.

Heidi was brash and impulsive and she didn't take life at all seriously.

And the woman standing before him was…not as he had always pictured her. Her light brown hair fell in waves at her bare shoulders, and her tank top showed off a tight figure that wasn't shy on the curves. But it was that smile that disarmed him the most. Big and joyful, that seemed to spread all the way up to those bright eyes that held a hint of challenge in them.

"You know what I mean. This is probably the most we've ever spoken to each other in our lives."

"It is," Heidi said with a nod. "Look, the cottage has two bedrooms. We can each take one and start looking for another rental. Whoever finds one first, moves out. And we split the rent."

He raised an eyebrow at that. Splitting the rent could come in handy, especially when he'd projected that the next month or so would be lean here at the pub. And if he started looking for a new place today, he might be able to move in by the first of next month. Surely something would pop up by then.

Of course, he'd prefer to stay.

"Are you actually going to look for a new place?" he wanted to know.

She seemed startled. "Are you actually willing to agree to this arrangement?"

"I don't think we have much choice. Unless you plan to let me have it."

She gave a little smirk. "Nice try. And yes, I will talk to Lanie about finding me another place to live. Until then, I guess I'll see you at home?"

She jingled the keys that he knew didn't belong to that luxury sedan she'd clearly borrowed from a family member and pushed off from the counter, giving a full view of those long, tanned legs.

Ryan swallowed hard, saying nothing, because really what was there to say?

He cleared his throat and turned to the men at the end of the bar, who did a good job of pretending they hadn't overheard everything, but at least he knew they weren't part of the local gossip mill. Their interests were simpler than that, mostly centered on fishing, beer, and watching sports, in his bar. He'd take it.

"Another round, gentlemen?" He didn't wait for their response before pulling the tap, but he kept one corner of his eye out the window, watching as his new housemate slid her oversized sunglasses down over her face and tucked into the driver's seat.

For over a year, he'd kept his world small, on purpose. Devoted himself to this bar. To making it better. To giving himself a purpose.

It had been lonely at times. It had been challenging, but boring too in a way. He'd had a routine. He'd kept it simple.

And now, everything was about to get very interesting. And he didn't know how he felt about that. He only knew he didn't have much of a choice, did he?

3

"How's the new house?" Bella asked two days later when Heidi showed up for her first shift since the move.

Heidi hung her messenger bag on the coat rack and then bent to greet her sister's golden retriever puppy, who was growing bigger by the day. As usual, George happily accepted the ear scratches and then rolled onto his back, paws waving in invitation for a belly rub.

Heidi laughed, but the tension was still evident in her voice.

"It's...okay." She rose, wincing at the worried pinch to Bella's brow. No doubt Bella had been expecting a problem; no doubt they all were. For this reason, Heidi had been quick to return her mother's car on Wednesday and grab her bike from the garage before she was spotted.

But now the truth was going to come out. A part of Heidi was surprised that it hadn't already spread like wildfire, as gossip tended to do in Blue Harbor. Bella and Brooke were close; though not close enough for Bella to know about their cousin's growing family. No, that was a secret that only Ryan knew about, and now, well, her.

It was a bond, she supposed. Along with the shared living quarters.

"There was a bit of a...mix-up." Heidi evaded her

sister's stare and grabbed a stack of books that had just arrived. They were the newest release from a popular author, and she and Bella wouldn't have to argue about a prominent display. "Do you want these on the new release table? Although, I was thinking I could refresh the window this afternoon, maybe build something around this? I'll get started on some ideas." She made haste to walk away, but Bella stopped her.

"Uh-uh. None of that." Bella's tone was one of warning. "I'm not your boss right now, I'm your sister, and the books can wait. What's going on?"

She was cornered. With a huff, Heidi set the stack down again and gave a shrug as she met her sister's gaze. "It seems that someone else also leased the cottage."

There was a beat of silence as Bella's frown grew deeper. "Someone else? How is that even possible?"

"Crazy, isn't it?" Heidi hoped to keep her tone breezy, even though the situation was far from a laughing matter. She'd ended up in the room she'd thought would be her spare—for what use, she hadn't been sure of when she'd first seen the place, and she was embarrassed to admit even to herself that she'd floated the fantasy of a home office space, one where she could build her marketing business that Bella had encouraged her to consider. One that she really wanted to pursue, if she could just muster up the courage to do it. But that required time, and right now she had actual problems to deal with.

But more than that, it would require other people. People who would be willing to give her a chance—or a second chance, for most.

"But you signed the lease through Lanie, right?"

There it was. The hint of suspicion. The assumption that Heidi had messed up, not followed the rules, somehow played an active part in her own misfortune.

"Yes, I used Lanie to handle the lease," she said, noting the bitter edge that had crept into her voice. "The other renter went directly through the owners of the property, but Lanie assured me that my lease was legitimate."

She gave her sister a hard stare because she couldn't help but resent that Lanie's word counted more than her own.

Even if she had rightfully earned the reputation she was now trying so hard to undo.

Bella must have picked up on her hurt because her expression softened when she shook her head. "Then I'm sure it's all fine. Lanie will sort it out. And you are still living there? You moved in?"

"Moved in. Living there." Heidi nodded. Just not alone, she thought. She pulled in a breath, her mind running through a few ways of phrasing the delivery of the real news, when the door jangled and Lanie swept in, looking chic and neat as always in her very adult shift dress as opposed to Heidi's jeans and peasant blouse.

Heidi made a note to go shopping for some similar items this weekend, especially now that she was saving half a month's rent. A small perk.

"I was hoping I'd find you here," Lanie said, dropping her gaze to give George a fond smile. His tail was beating so loudly that it was smacking the wall, making Heidi forget her troubles for a moment as they all laughed.

But when Lanie straightened up and turned her attention on Heidi, even Bella seemed to hold her breath. "I've been on the phone with the Tinleys. It took me a couple of days to reach them because they'd been on a cruise and were unreachable. They feel just awful about this mess."

Heidi's heart began to race. Surely, they would honor her lease, especially as Lanie had handled it, which couldn't be said for the other party.

"They'll let me stay, won't they?"

Lanie nodded, but the look on her face told Heidi that the news wasn't all good. "They don't see how they can ask either of you to give up the lease, since they did technically promise you each the space."

"Wait," Bella cut in. "Who's the other person? We didn't get to that part yet."

Lanie raised an eyebrow. This was Heidi's news to deliver.

"Ryan Harrison," she mumbled, now grabbing that stack of books that Bella had insisted could wait. No, it couldn't wait.

Bella didn't look particularly moved by this announcement. "Well, Ryan's pretty reasonable. I'm sure he'll understand that you have a lease through a real estate agent."

Reasonable? Heidi curled her lip and set a few of the books on the new release table, rearranging others to make space. She could think of several choice words to describe Ryan and none were half as generous. But then, Bella mostly kept to herself, either with her head in a book when they were growing up, or here in the store when she got

older. Ryan was just a passing face in their crowd, but the bigger part, Heidi knew, was that Ryan had very little reason to give any reaction to Bella.

Whereas he'd always given Heidi a creeping sense of disdain. There were the weddings, of course, where he sat like a lump, watching everyone else mingle and dance. And the holiday events in town, where he chose to judge the activities rather than participate in the fun. She could still remember his face when she'd come down the sledding hill last December, yes, squealing as loudly as her niece Zoe, who was sharing her sled. His gaze seemed to cut through the cold winter afternoon, as cold as ice.

"But technically, Ryan has a legitimate lease too. Directly with the owner." Lanie sighed deeply. "I'm afraid you'll have to decide which of you will be the one to move out."

"Move out?" Bella's voice rose a notch and she turned to Heidi with wide eyes. "You mean, he's living there too?"

Heidi grimaced. "As Lanie said, he technically signed a lease."

"And how's that going to work?" Bella asked.

"Good question." Heidi hadn't seen Ryan since their conversation at the pub the other day. His hours were long, starting early and ending late, and Heidi did have a tendency to sleep in on her days off, which her sisters and parents were forever commenting on, of course. His shampoo and razor were in the bathroom, right beside her ample stash of beauty and hair supplies. His blue towel hung beside her pink one. Of course, his was perfectly folded and draped, like a hotel maid had tended to it.

The only way she knew Ryan was still even staying in the house was because she'd gone to bed early, closing herself into her room both nights, hearing him come in before she'd managed to fall asleep, hoping that she didn't snore loud enough to be heard through the walls. No doubt he'd reprimand her for that, or give her one of those long, unimpressed stares like he had at Britt and Robbie's wedding in May when she'd danced with her niece Zoe at the reception, silly, slightly clumsy moves that had made the little girl giggle until she started hiccupping. And yes, they'd removed their shoes. But the reception had been outdoors at the Conway Orchard and Winery, and her heels would have sunk into the grass otherwise!

Ryan had sat off to the side, at one of the singles tables, talking to no one, certainly not dancing with anyone. She'd only even noticed him because she'd caught him looking at her a few times while she twirled Zoe (and then had Zoe twirl her, which was admittedly awkward).

Now, she wondered just how panicked he would have been if she'd run over and grabbed his hands and dragged him out onto the dance floor, ignoring all protests. The man probably would have had a heart attack. And thirty-five-year-olds could have them, right?

"Why are you smiling?" Bella asked.

Heidi blinked. "Oh, I was just thinking about the fact that at least I'll be saving half a month's rent."

"You can't honestly be planning to stay there!" Bella stared at her.

Heidi shrugged. "Why not stay for now? Ryan's…"

"A decent enough guy," Bella said begrudgingly, and Lanie nodded her agreement.

Heidi opened her eyes wide but said nothing. That was hardly what she'd been about to say, but she didn't see much point in discussing it.

"Ryan's quiet. Mostly keeps to himself. But you never knew him that well, Heidi. With your age difference," Bella said.

"The age difference is barely noticeable now," Heidi said tersely. Honestly, her sister was intent to still treat her like a child sometimes! "Besides, I knew Ryan, of course."

Knew enough to decide that she didn't like him.

"Regardless of how harmless he is, there must be some other place one of you could move into?" Bella looked at Lanie who shook her head.

"This time of year? It's lake season, and you know what that means."

They did. The whole town did. It meant that the sidewalks were filled with tourists from Chicago and other big Midwestern cities. The inns had been booked out for months. The rental properties too.

"It won't be easy, but if someone has a last-minute change of plans, something could pop up. I'll let you know. Ryan probably has the same idea, because he called and asked me to stop by the pub today."

Heidi didn't know why that stung. Ryan wanted to find a different place. One that he didn't have to share with her. It wasn't personal, obviously, but somehow it felt like it was.

He didn't even know her. Maybe, he didn't want to try. Maybe, like most people in town, he already had ideas about her, even if they were unfair.

"Thanks, Lanie," Heidi said. She picked up the remaining books and brought them back to the counter, waiting for the inevitable advice that her sister was itching to dole out.

"You sure this is going to be okay? My apartment is small, but you're always welcome to the sofa." There was a worried pinch between Bella's eyebrows, one that Heidi hadn't seen since the shop was in trouble over the spring.

Sleeping on Bella's couch was the last thing Heidi wanted to do. It would mean she wasn't capable of solving her own problems. It would mean that once again, she was relying on her family members to take care of her.

"I'm fine," she said firmly. "Lanie will probably find something, even if it's not ideal. And in the meantime…"

In the meantime, she'd just use the opportunity to get to know Ryan a little better. Or avoid him as best she could.

*

Her stuff was everywhere. Ryan closed the door to the cottage behind him and stared at the transformation of the living room, which he'd quite liked up until this moment. Now, the basic beige pillows on the couch had been replaced with floral ones, and there was a soft blue blanket flung over the back of the armchair. On the coffee table, a spread of magazines had appeared, along with a vase filled with flowers he couldn't name and didn't like, because that's where he'd prefer to set his plate while he ate his microwavable dinner in front of the television—on the nights that he managed to leave the pub at a decent hour, at least.

From the hallway, he heard the sound of the water

rushing in the shower, but there was another sound, one that made him pause and listen for a moment. Singing. A woman singing.

She had a surprisingly good voice.

The water stopped and Ryan stiffened, feeling uncomfortable. He moved quickly to the kitchen, where he halted in the doorway, taking in the sight. There were more flowers on the small table in the nook near the window. And on the windowsill behind the sink, where he'd stuck a roll of paper towels, was a row of what he could only suppose were herbs judging from the color.

Gingerly, he crossed the room and bent over to smell them. Yep. Herbs. And now his roll of paper towels had been stuck in some wrought-iron contraption that would make tearing one off that much more of a process.

A tingle of a memory he'd worked hard to push from his mind threatened to break through the surface. Since coming back to Blue Harbor last year, he'd made a point not to date, but to focus on the practical side of his life instead—God knew the pub kept him busy enough.

And now…

His eyes slid to the range, where a floral-printed hand towel was hanging from the oven handlebar. Now he had floral hand towels.

"Oh!"

He turned to see Heidi, looking startled in the doorway to the kitchen. Her hair was damp and loose at her shoulders, creating wet splotches on the thin fabric of her pink tee shirt. She was wearing pajama pants with—you guessed it—flowers on them, and her toenails were painted a pale shade of blue that for some reason made him stare longer than he probably should have. There was something about this girl—make that woman—he corrected himself, that both intrigued and unsettled him all at once.

"You're home."

The way she so casually said the word made him take pause, but he decided not to correct her. Technically, this was her home as much as his, at least for the short term, but the way she'd said it made it feel like a shared habitat, something more than a house with two bedrooms, and a kitchen…full of flowers.

He hadn't shared a home with anyone since his last relationship ended—and that day had been one he'd chosen to forget. Or at least, not think about it.

"I think I'm home," he said, glancing back at the flowers that consumed a fair portion of the small table's surface. It was no bother, really, since he ate most of his meals on the couch in front of the television, or lately, at his desk back at the pub, in front of a computer screen.

"I thought I'd cozy the place up a bit. Make it feel homier. Those flowers are from the yard. They were so beautiful, I didn't see how I couldn't pick them, especially since I don't know the first thing about gardening." She blinked at him with those wide blue eyes that allowed no space for criticism or suggestion.

"It looks nice," he said. And he supposed it did, not that he paid attention to things like pillows or blankets or…flowers. No, what he cared about was everyday life. The stuff that got you from the start to the finish line in one piece. The stuff that mattered.

The stuff he could control. Except lately, he didn't have anything under control. He couldn't figure out the basic essentials that could take his family's pub from death's door to a big success. It had been riding on fumes for years, and while he'd once thought it was his brother's doing, he knew now that Kyle had done the best he could with the place he'd taken over from their late father.

Certainly, a better job than Ryan, despite his big plans and even greater efforts.

"I like the…herbs," he said because Heidi was still giving him that hopeful look. "You must cook a lot."

A flush crept up her cheeks and she hesitated before saying, "Sometimes. I grabbed a bite in town today, though."

"Oh? Where?" He liked to know these things for research purposes, but Heidi gave him a funny look in return. One that made him wary. One that told him he might have come across as interested in more than where she'd spent her money, when he absolutely was not.

Sure, Heidi was pretty. Wavy hair and those bright eyes, and a smile that, well, almost pulled a smile from him. But she was just a kid. His sister-in-law Brooke's younger cousin. Her baby cousin. He could still remember the way Heidi and Jenna had behaved at his brother's wedding all those years back. Like two teenagers who couldn't stop giggling.

Looking back, they probably were just barely in their twenties at the time.

"Firefly Café," Heidi answered.

Ryan nodded. The Firefly Café was owned by Amelia

Conway, soon to be Bradford now that she and Matt were recently engaged. Amelia was also his sister-in-law's cousin on the other side of her family, and even though Amelia and Heidi weren't related by blood, all the Conway and Clark girls were as close as sisters. Confident, giggly, and admittedly, a little intimidating, at least in his younger days.

He glanced at Heidi warily as she opened the freezer and helped herself to a pint of ice cream that she'd already written her name on in thick black ink. He watched in mild horror as she opened a drawer, retrieved a spoon, and stuck it square in the middle of the container.

Things like this made him twitch. His brother would have just had a good laugh and told him to loosen up. It was also probably why Kyle was happily married with a baby on the way while Ryan, four years his senior, spent most of his time in a dark office with a dying fig plant as his sole companion.

What was Rex Tinley thinking asking him to tend to the plants in this old cottage? What had Rex Tinley been thinking handing him that lease while his wife was handing Lanie and Heidi the other copy?

"You don't ever get into the pub," he said, again regretting his choice of words when she flashed him a look and then gave a slow smile before cramming a spoonful of ice cream into her mouth.

"Firefly Café is more my scene. Except when Candy's working."

Ryan swallowed back a smile. Candy Conway had arrived in town before he came back, and she made the personalities of the other Conway and Clark women seem small by comparison.

Panic made Ryan's pulse kick when he thought about the secret he'd let slip. Candy tended to get overexcited about things. She'd played a big part in her stepdaughter's recent wedding and she'd no doubt start decorating a nursery the moment she heard that her step-niece and Ryan's brother were expecting a baby.

"About what I let slip the other day…"

"You mean about Brooke being pregnant? Don't worry, I only told Candy. You know how she is. She sniffed me out. She can almost smell when someone's holding back a juicy piece of gossip. It was pointless to insist otherwise."

Ryan felt himself pale. He and his brother hadn't had the best relationship growing up, and it had been equally shaky when he'd arrived back in town and Kyle thought he was stepping on his toes. It was only in recent months that they'd started to form a strong bond, as adults, and equals, even if Kyle was starting to feel like more of the grown-up these days.

"You didn't," he whispered.

"You're right. I didn't." Heidi grinned and scooped out another chunk of ice cream. She chewed thoughtfully, then said, "You didn't actually *believe* I'd do that, did you?"

"I don't know…I don't really know you," he said, even though he felt he had a fairly good handle on her personality. It was big, and bold, and left him on uneven footing. He couldn't tell when she was joking or serious, and he was, admittedly, always serious. Kyle had teased him about that growing up. A lot of kids had.

She shrugged. "Well, you're about to get to know me. Seeing as we're living together."

Living together. Ryan watched Heidi slip back into the living room. A moment later, the television flickered on and a dating reality show filled the screen. He'd been looking forward to relaxing in front of the evening news for a while, hearing what was happening in the world.

It was Friday night. Mitch was manning the bar tonight, and unless he wanted to go in and try the menu for the umpteenth time, each time feeling frustrated when someone asked for something off the old menu instead, he had the option of ordering a pizza or heading out.

He didn't make it a habit to frequent the competition, but right now, he could use a friend, and Jackson Bradford was sure to be tending bar.

*

Fifteen minutes later, Ryan slid into a seat at the bar of the Carriage House Inn's pub, trying to push aside the anxiety that rose when he looked around at the crowded space. Not a table was empty. The fire was flickering invitingly in the hearth, even though it was well into June, and there were groups of happy people of all ages, eating, drinking, enjoying their location of choice.

He checked his feelings immediately. When his father had started Harrison's Pub, he'd established it as a local watering hole. A no-frills place where local fishermen came for a drink after a long day on Lake Huron. There was beer and there was liquor, and there was the occasional bottle of wine (Conway blend, of course, because long before Kyle married Brooke Conway, the family was supporting the local winery). The menu had been simple and just as

limited. Basic bar food with none of the extras. The place had been dark, but not exactly cozy. There had never been a fireplace or candles on the tables, and when he'd taken things over last summer, done a light renovation to clean up the joint, and then revamped the menu—make that attempted to revamp the menu—he'd been met with resistance.

Kyle had been right. His kid brother, whom he'd assumed had done a poor job of carrying on their father's legacy, had actually known what he was doing all along, even if his heart had never been in it. He'd given the people what they wanted, but the problem was there weren't half as many people coming to Harrison's as there were coming to this place.

"Well, this is a nice surprise. You're not working tonight?" Jackson flung the bar cloth over his shoulder and set two firm hands on the polished counter, which only served to remind Ryan that he really needed to upgrade the one at Harrison's, which was faded and nicked from decades of use.

Maybe, decades of love, or so Kyle had told him, and their father before that.

"I think the place can survive one night without me," he said, hearing the irony in his own words. The place had survived without him for long enough—or at least, hung on by a thread. But was his mark on it for the better or the detriment? He still wasn't sure.

"Beer?" Jackson didn't wait for the answer before pouring Ryan a Guinness. Their acquaintanceship went way back to their school days. They'd grown up together, and they both had brothers married to Conways.

That was where the comparisons ended. While Jackson was extroverted and energetic, always happy to float from one casual relationship to another, never taking life too seriously, Ryan had always taken it a little too seriously, first with grades, then with college, later with his job, and then… Well, no sense counting his long-term relationship that hadn't ended in marriage as he'd intended.

And of course, there was no comparing this pub with his own. He and Jackson had both taken over the establishments from their parents, but one was booming, with a line of people waiting for entry, and the other…Ryan could almost picture the regular crowd at his bar. Other than the occasional frat boys or bachelor nights, it was mostly a middle-aged or older crowd of widowers or loners, looking for a little company but not much conversation.

Ryan skimmed the menu, wondering again why people were willing to order this type of food here but not down the street at Harrison's. He settled on the house burger on the pretzel roll. Simple, but expertly seasoned. The fries were always made to perfection.

"Kyle joining you tonight?" Jackson asked after he put in the order and helped two young women, both pretty, and both clearly smitten by his grin and a wink as he poured them their white wine.

"Nah, he's doing the whole married life thing." And soon he'd be doing the family life. Ryan was looking forward to being an uncle even if he didn't have much experience with kids. At the rate he was going, it might be the closest thing he ever got to having one of his own.

"Same with Robbie." Jackson grinned when he spoke of his younger brother. "Sometimes it sounds nice."

Ryan sputtered on his drink. "Hold on a minute. Are you saying that you're suddenly interested in the whole white picket fence lifestyle?"

"There are a lot of white picket fences in Blue Harbor," Jackson said thoughtfully. He shrugged. "I'll never say never. What about you?"

Ryan took a long sip of his drink. Other than Kyle, no one knew about his breakup back in Cleveland, the one that made him reconsider his life choices up to that point, the one that had brought him back here. He'd closed himself off to the possibility of love for over a year, but could he say never again?

Probably not.

"Never say never," he agreed. "But right now, I have a lot to sort out first."

Jackson's grin turned knowing. "Ah yes. I heard about your current living situation."

That news had certainly flown fast, but then, this was Blue Harbor, Jackson was equally linked to the Conways through Robbie's wife Britt, and, by default, the Clarks. The leak could have come from a number of sources.

He was surprised his own brother hadn't texted him yet, but it was just a matter of time. Possibly hours.

"How'd you hear?" He could only shake his head. "Let me guess. Bella?"

"Bella and I don't exactly hang out, especially now that she's canoodling with that famous author boyfriend."

True, and Bella had always been reserved, even when they were kids. She certainly had a softer nature than her younger sister.

His mind flitted back to the image of Heidi, curled up on the armchair that he had actually moved over from his old apartment, that soft throw blanket over her long legs, the pint of ice cream in one hand.

She'd offered him some on his way out that door, but that seemed a little germy and, the bigger problem, far too intimate.

Heidi was unpredictable. Outgoing. Easygoing. Everything he wasn't.

Really, she was a lot like the guy standing on the other side of the bar.

For some reason, though, the thought of Jackson making a move on Heidi bothered him, giving him a strange pull in his gut that even a long sip of beer didn't dissolve.

Besides, Heidi was far too young for Jackson. She'd still been a little girl in pigtails when he and Jackson were entering high school!

"Don't tell me it was Candy Conway," Ryan said flatly, even though she was bound to find out, and comment on it. He liked to keep his distance from the woman, even though that wasn't always feasible. She made Jackson look like a wallflower. Heidi, too.

"No, but good guess." Jackson paused as he took a plate from a server and set it before Ryan. Immediately, Ryan saw the difference between the food here and back at Harrison's. The Carriage House Inn was authentic. Their service was effortless. While Harrison's was trying to figure out its identity. Maybe, it was trying too hard to be something it wasn't and could never be.

Much like himself, he thought sadly.

"I heard it from Lanie, actually. She was in here earlier with some of the girls."

Ryan didn't need to ask if they'd planned to head over to Harrison's afterward. When a woman walked into the place, what little conversation there was tended to stop for a moment until the locals recovered from their shock.

"So, Heidi Clark? How's that working out?" The gleam in Jackson's eyes was undeniable.

Ryan munched on some fries, groaning at both how perfectly cooked and seasoned they were and how much better than were than the ones his cook was frying up. "Well, there are pink towels in my bathroom and flowers on every available surface. I might need to install a padlock on my bedroom door."

"You don't plan to open that door?" Jackson cocked a mischievous eyebrow.

"Please," Ryan scoffed through a mouth full of his burger. "She's a kid."

"Not really," Jackson pointed out.

Ryan let that sink in for a moment, picturing that curvy body, the way she'd so expertly put him in his place at the bar the other day, holding out those papers and spelling things out for him.

No, Ryan supposed she wasn't a kid anymore. But he couldn't think of her as anything else. Could he?

4

When Bella suggested that they have a "sisters lunch" the next day, Heidi knew that a lecture was coming. It wasn't often that all three of the Clark girls met, especially since Natalie worked out on Evening Island and ferried across the lake each day, and Bella didn't like to leave the shop closed for long, either. An exception had therefore been made, clearly meaning there was an important topic to discuss. The question was, would it be about her living situation, her job situation, or both?

Warily, Heidi stepped away from the window display that she'd finished arranging, this time with summer vibes, right down to some sand and rocks and some colorful beach totes, stuffed with the latest paperbacks, their titles visible at the top, of course.

"Who's going to watch the store?" she said by way of excuse.

Bella shrugged. "One of the perks of being the owner is that I can turn the sign when I need to and if someone really wants to buy something, they can pop back a little later. Come on, we can go to Buttercream Bakery. I'm craving a chocolate cupcake today."

Nice try with the bribery. It wasn't lost on her. Still, Heidi perked up at the mention of Maddie Conway's sweets, even though she needed to know what she walking into first. "Isn't Natalie working today?"

"Nope. She has the day off. I guess they're going through some staffing changes this summer."

Heidi frowned at that, knowing that, as a single mother, their sister relied on a steady income, but Bella didn't seem to think anything of it, so Heidi shelved the possibility that their lunch could be about someone other than her. The eldest of the Clarks, Natalie worked at the island's big, historic hotel that was only open from spring through fall. Come winter, she stayed on the mainland, working just down the street at Cora Conway's holiday shop.

She'd never complained about her job before. Never hinted at any trouble, either. The arrangement worked for her and her daughter, and unlike Heidi, her work had remained consistent over the years.

"Zoe's at art camp and it would be nice for us all to get together. We don't do it enough."

No, they didn't. Even though they all lived in town, their proximity sometimes made them take advantage of their closeness. There was always tomorrow. Always another weekend. But the days went by, and more and more, Heidi only saw Natalie in passing, or when they got together with the Conways for a bigger event. Natalie's free time was limited, and unlike Heidi, and until recently, Bella, Natalie still made time to date, even if it hadn't yet led to the relationship she was hoping to find.

"Okay. But what about George?"

"Craig is going to take him for a long walk to the pond today." Bella looked at her strangely. "Are you trying to avoid me?"

Heidi hedged her bets on an honest answer. "Maybe. I'm a little worried that I'm walking into an ambush."

Bella looked surprised. "Over what? Unless there's something you haven't shared with us?"

Heidi gave her sister a frank look. "You see me almost every day. My life is an open book, pun intended," she remarked.

"In that case, let's head out. Natalie is probably already waiting for us, and I told Craig I'd hand off George on our way there. He was writing all morning," Bella added with a little smile that was new to her face, reminding Heidi that her sister—her very quiet and content sister—had found a spark in her otherwise routine days. She was in love, even if she might not have proclaimed it out loud. But Heidi was happy for her. Craig was a good match for her—they had a lot in common, and not just their love of books and George.

Whereas Heidi and Ryan... She shook her head while they let themselves out of the store, Bella passing her George's lead so she could lock the door behind her. Ryan was about as different from Heidi as a man could be. She'd seen the way he carefully rolled his toothpaste tube. The way he wiped down the sink after each use. Just this morning, when she'd walked into the living room, she'd seen that he had folded up the throw blanket and draped it over the back of the armchair sometime between last night and this morning. If she didn't know better, she'd say he'd plumped the pillows too.

He was a neat freak to her messy streak. He was quiet to her robust energy. He was reserved while she, as

evidenced last night, sometimes couldn't stop talking, especially when she was nervous.

He was an adult. And she...she was about to be lectured over lunch by her two older sisters.

She just knew it.

*

Natalie was already waiting for them at a corner table inside when Heidi and Bella pushed through the door into the sweet-smelling shop, her loose curls falling casually over her shoulder in a low ponytail. Heidi's stomach grumbled when she took in the overflowing baskets of fresh blueberry muffins and scones that sat on top of the glass display case. She let her eyes rest on the cinnamon crumb cake that was housed behind a glass dome and decided that coming here had been a good idea—even if she was most certainly about to be ambushed. She may as well make it worth her while.

"Hello, ladies." Maddie smiled as they approached the counter, and waved her hand like a game show host to the baskets of goodies. "What will it be today? And don't even tell me that you'll have your usual, Bella," she joked.

Bella's cheeks turned pink. "Am I that predictable?"

Heidi almost balked at that, because there were few people as organized and regimented as Bella. And she could now say that she'd lived with both of them.

"A rosemary scone and a vanilla latte? Yes." Maddie laughed. "Heidi, you, on the other hand, are always full of surprises."

That much was true, and Maddie should know. Being

the youngest in her family had brought her and Heidi close, and though their mutual cousin Jenna was about their age, she had always been quieter by nature.

Today, though, Heidi didn't get the sense that Maddie was referring to the time that she'd dared her to skinny dip...in April. Or even what Heidi might select from the selection of baked goods.

There was a twinkle in her eye that told Heidi this had everything to do with her current living situation. Or predicament.

"If you're referring to my housemate, I can assure you that no one was as surprised as I was."

Maddie did a poor job of hiding her smile as she went to work on Bella's latte. Over the sound of the machine foaming the milk, she said, "Oh, I can think of one person. Ryan couldn't have taken the news well."

That was an understatement. Still, there was no denying that things weren't as bad as Heidi had feared they could be. Ryan was surprisingly easygoing, at least as far as roommates went, and she'd had enough over the years to appreciate that he rinsed out his cereal bowl in the morning rather than dropping it in the sink like her old roommate had, leaving the remaining bits to grow soggy in the leftover milk.

"It's only temporary," Heidi said firmly. "We're both looking for new places, and Lanie promised to tell us when something pops up."

"Well, you certainly know how to make life interesting for yourself, Heidi," Maddie said as she slid the steaming mug to Bella. "But if that guy gives you any trouble, you be sure to let us know."

Heidi couldn't help but laugh. "Ryan? Trouble?" The man was far too uptight to ever get in any sort of trouble. Besides, she wasn't the teenage girl who caved under his disapproving stare anymore. She was a grown woman, even if the arch look on Natalie's face from across the room didn't say as much.

"I'll have a slice of that crumb cake, please. And a regular coffee," she sighed, thinking that she'd really prefer a glass of wine about now.

"I'll bring it all over to you. Natalie looks impatient," Maddie noted.

Bella lifted her mug and took a sip, leaving a line of foam from her latte on her top lip. A convenient excuse not to have to argue that point, no doubt.

Shoulders heavy with dread, Heidi trudged over to the back of the room, where Natalie was sipping an iced tea. She pushed aside a chair as they approached, clearing away her cell phone and tucking it into her tote bag.

"I assume you've heard as well," Heidi said.

"The whole town has heard," Natalie remarked, her blue eyes bright. It was the one feature that identified them as sisters because their personalities couldn't be much more different.

Heidi glanced at Bella, retracting that thought.

Heidi wished she didn't still worry about these things, but she couldn't help it. "You mean Mom and Dad know too?"

"I just saw Mom this morning when she came to pick up Zoe for camp. I mentioned it only because I assumed Candy had gotten to her by now. Miraculously, she hadn't, but now the news is out." She tipped her head, giving a cajoling smile. "Come on, it was bound to reach her sooner than later."

Heidi grimaced. She hadn't checked her phone since leaving the house this morning, but now she could only assume there would be a string of texts and voicemails. Gratefully, she looked up to see Maddie approaching with a mug and a plate holding a thick slab of cake.

Sensing the tension, Maddie handed it to her and then went quickly back to the counter.

"There's no *news*. It's a basic misunderstanding," Heidi said through a mouthful of the buttery cake. "Not some scandal. Besides, Lanie is handling it."

"And until she does?" Natalie lifted an eyebrow.

Bella set down her mug and licked her lip. "If she doesn't find anything, you could be sharing that house for…weeks. Months. Why don't you reconsider staying with me for a while, until you find something new?"

"And let Ryan take my house?" Heidi stared at her sisters. "I don't think so."

Natalie frowned deeply. "I thought you said that you were looking for something else."

"I am," Heidi said quickly. "I mean, I said I am and…I am. But so is Ryan, and I just don't see why I should be the one to have to move out. I found that house, I signed a lease, and I plan to live there."

Her sisters exchanged a glance. One that told her the adults were talking, that they were judging her, most likely deciding who would take the role of good cop and who would play bad cop.

As a kid, the roles usually pertained to birth order, but now that Bella was Heidi's boss, she tended to extend that role to their personal lives at times. Today was likely no exception.

Heidi decided to cut them off before they could start on her. "I have it figured out. It's no big deal. Besides, you all know Ryan. He's completely harmless."

And annoying, and smug, and absolutely no fun.

There was nothing they could argue about there, so, with resigned looks and heavy shrugs, they said nothing more.

"Believe it or not, I know what I'm doing," Heidi said, but there was a hesitation in her voice despite its defensive edge.

"We never said you didn't," Bella said gently.

"No? Well, it's always implied." Heidi set down her coffee. "Look, I know I've messed up a lot in the past, but those days are behind me. I have a good job now." She darted her eyes from Bella. They both knew that position was part-time and would remain that way, too. "And I have this lovely little house. I'm getting settled. So I have an unexpected roommate. It's just for the time being. At least I'm saving on rent for a while, right?"

Again, they could only murmur their consent, and Heidi decided that she should feel grateful for small favors. It wasn't like her sisters were trying to set her up with Ryan or insinuate that more could develop with them. They'd probably leave that conversation to Candy.

Because only Candy would be crazy enough to come up with a notion like that.

Her phone pinged: an unusual occurrence at this time of day, given that all of her cousins and friends were working and her boss was technically sitting right beside her.

"How much do you want to bet that this text is from Mom?"

Natalie held up her hands under Heidi's hard glare. "I said I was sorry. Besides, wasn't the news better coming from me than from Candy? I can only imagine how that woman might have spun it."

True, but Heidi wasn't going to let her sister off the hook that easily.

Seeing no reason to put off the inevitable, she pulled her phone from her bag and checked the screen, her pulse quickening when she saw the text from Lanie.

"All your concerns might be over by the end of the day anyway," she told her sisters now, as she stood to go. "Lanie found another listing. A rental that fell through at the final hour. See? Nothing to worry about."

Only her smile felt tight as she swung her bag over her shoulder. She knew she should be happy to have this problem solved for her so quickly, but for some reason, she wasn't. And she wasn't exactly sure why that was.

*

The call from Lanie came shortly after Ryan had finished arranging the furniture in the office space over the pub. Cole McCarthy and his crew had worked late into the day yesterday, and he could see the progress already. He crossed the room—a vast improvement over the dark, cramped workspace below—and lifted his phone from his desk. Relief swept through him when he read the text.

He wasted no time in jogging down the stairs, coughing at the dust that had built up with the ongoing construction. He surveyed the main floor of the pub now, happy to see that a new wall was going up, pushed back deeper into the space, where he'd relocate the pool table, separating the games from the main dining area. But as he pushed through the tarp into the bar, his good spirits sank when he took in the crowd. The same lonely old widowers sat hunched over on their stools, nursing their beers, one eye on the television. Sure, it was only afternoon, but it was also, as Lanie had mentioned again in her text, lake season, and that meant there was an influx of people to Blue Harbor for four straight months; summer people who'd stick around all summer, and tourists who came up for a weekend or a week at a time.

There was no doubt in his mind that if he strolled by the Carriage House Inn right now, there'd be groups of young people, enjoying a summer afternoon, sipping drinks and munching on snacks, laughing and talking, not staring gloomily at a television screen.

It was probably too late to pull in a crowd for this year, but maybe, with some imagination, he could figure out a way to make things different by next year. If he could keep things afloat until then.

Deciding that he didn't have time to worry about that at the moment, he signaled to his bartender as he crossed to the door. "I'll be back in about an hour. Maybe we can go over the new menu ideas when I get back?"

Mitch shrugged, but it was old Lenny who curled a lip and said, "Why do you want to keep on changing this place? First with pulling back those shades and letting all this light in, and then with these new-fangled lanterns. You've fiddled with that menu more times than I can count." He turned to get a good look at Ryan, pointing a gnarled finger. "Your father built this place around the customers, not trends, and your brother had the good sense to stay loyal to that. I thought you were supposed to be the smart one?"

Ryan felt his jaw twitch. He told himself the guy had been drinking, that he was old and set in his ways, but the words still stung, because they were true. He was supposed to be the smart one, at least in the academic sense. While Kyle had been artistic and creative, it was Ryan who had put his nose in the books and made the honor roll each quarter. Ryan who had prioritized attending a good college, and securing a corporate job after graduation. And it was Kyle who had kept this place running, just as their father would have wanted.

But his father wouldn't have wanted to see this place fall by the wayside. And that was exactly what would have happened eventually if Ryan hadn't stepped in. The margins were better, but not good enough.

"We'll talk when you get back," Mitch called out, giving him a knowing look. One that said he got it, that there was no reason to pay any credence to Lenny, even if he was an old-timer, a regular, and the antithesis of the crowd that Ryan was looking to draw.

And that was exactly the reason why Ryan should listen to him, he thought as he pushed outside.

He checked the address that Lanie had texted him,

pleased that it was within walking distance. He noted the time on his phone and walked at his usual pace so he could clock his commute and factor it into his decision. When he arrived at the house at the opposite end of town from the cottage, he noted the time again. Three minutes farther. Six each day. Not a deal-breaker, exactly. Still, little details added up.

The house itself was nondescript. Wooden, painted white like many houses in the town, with a small gate and two front doors, meaning it was a multi-unit residence. One of the doors opened now and Lanie popped her head around, her expression lifting when she saw Ryan coming up the brick-paved path.

"Ryan, thank you for meeting me on such short notice. I'm still waiting on Heidi, but I can take you in now if you're pressed for time?"

He frowned slightly. "Heidi's coming?"

"It seemed only fair," Lanie said.

Ryan nodded his head after a moment. He couldn't argue with that. "Let's go ahead in. I have to get back to work soon." With any hope, he could do a quick walk-through and sign the lease before Heidi ever arrived. If she even arrived.

Maybe it was uncharitable of him, but Blue Harbor was small, most people worked in small businesses that kept the economy going, and gossip swirled like the riptides in Lake Huron. It was common knowledge that Heidi had been let go from more than one job for her tardiness.

Lanie grimaced slightly, her hand still holding the doorknob protectively against her back. "Now, remember, it will look different once the cleaning crew has been in. And it isn't as furnished as the Tinleys' cottage, so you'd need to bring in some new pieces. But with a little TLC, it's a real charmer."

Ryan narrowed his gaze and grunted. "We'll see about that."

With what could only be described as a gulp, Lanie released the knob and the door creaked open. She stepped back onto the porch to let Ryan pass—or perhaps to breathe—he realized, stepping into the small entrance hall.

When Lanie said that it wasn't as furnished as the cottage, she should have said that it wasn't furnished at all. The pea-green wall-to-wall carpet was stained and threadbare, whereas the cottage had gleaming hardwood floors. The plastic blinds on the windows were ripped and crooked. The place was stifling hot and smelled of something foul. "Mothballs?"

He coughed into his hand and Lanie rushed across the room to the nearest window, grunting with effort as she tried to pry it open, even though it was clear from the woodwork that the thing had been painted shut years ago.

Suddenly she froze. "Oh. Here's Heidi now."

She pulled in a big breath and then coughed into her hand, before hurrying to the door where her sales voice could be heard across the small space. "Heidi! Welcome. Now…"

Ryan managed to smile when he heard her reciting the same pitch to Heidi. For a moment, he felt sorry for her. Especially since there was no way that he was going to be the one taking this place.

"I can't wait to see— Oh."

Ryan turned to see Heidi standing in the entranceway, a tense Lanie grimacing behind her. From the way that Heidi's eyes swept the room, it was obvious that her disappointment—for once—wasn't at the sight of him.

"Welcome home!" He grinned, and she scowled at him. Deeply.

"When should I drop off your housewarming gift?" she quipped. "Tonight?"

Lanie teetered in on heels behind Heidi, who paused every few feet to sneeze.

"A little dust!" Lanie said brightly. "Nothing a good vacuum and mop can't spruce up. Why, if you pull the blinds and let the light in, you'll see that this place is really quite…charming."

Ryan secretly wondered when the definition of charming had changed to rundown, old, and smelly.

Lanie wrestled with the blinds to prove her point. Light filled the room, revealing even darker stains on the carpet, signs of obvious mold in the corners of the ceiling where water damage had been left untreated, and what was unmistakable evidence of a mouse.

Lanie and Heidi were now competing for whose look of horror was greatest, and Lanie began frantically lowering the blinds again, only managing to pull them from their clasps in the process. They clamored loudly to the carpet, igniting a cloud of dust that made her cough and then sneeze. And then sneeze again.

"This place should be condemned," Heidi said, and for once, Ryan had to agree with her. "I don't need to see the rest."

She marched back out onto the porch, and Lanie followed her. Ryan glimpsed into the mustard yellow and chocolate brown tiled bathroom and decided that he'd seen enough too.

"I'm going to be frank," Lanie said, once they were all on the porch. "This listing fell through this morning."

"Gee, I wonder why," Heidi remarked, crossing her arms.

Lanie blinked in surprise, and Ryan coughed into his hand to cover his laugh.

"Someone will take it by the end of the day," Lanie said. "In the right hands, it will be livable, trust me. And it's within walking distance of town and the lake. And need I stress this again, but it's—"

"Summer in Blue Harbor," Ryan and Heidi said at the same time.

He caught her eye, sensing a shared connection. It was brief, but it was there, and it sent a strange feeling through his chest.

"I'll leave you two to discuss things," Lanie said. "If one of you decides to take it, call or text me as soon as possible."

Ryan watched the real estate agent hurry down the path and let herself through the gate. He never knew a woman could move that quickly in high heels.

"Think she's running home to shower?" Heidi asked, glancing at him sidelong.

"At least to wash her hands," Ryan said, fighting off a smile. He looked at her squarely, about to lean onto the porch rail and rethinking that. Chances were high that it

would land him straight in the bushes. "What do you want to do about it?"

"This place?" Heidi scoffed. "Nothing. I can't imagine living here. And I don't have the money or time to fix it up."

"You expect me to live here then?"

She hesitated, long enough for him to realize she wasn't the selfish little girl he'd always thought her to be.

"You're in a better position to fix it up," she finally said.

"I'm already fixing up the pub." And doing a poor job at that. "I don't have the time for this sort of project either."

"What's our alternative then? You heard what Lanie said. We were lucky to find this place."

Worry shadowed her usually bright eyes. Her expression was so serious and the words were indeed true, that Ryan couldn't explain the sputter that came out of his mouth, making his shoulders shake until he was soon tossing his head back in laughter.

He laughed and laughed until his ribs ached, finally managing to compose himself as he set a hand to his stomach. "Sorry," he said, wiping the tears from his eyes. "I know it's not funny."

Except that it was. He wasn't sure when he'd ever forget that image of Heidi's face when she saw the mouse droppings. Or if he ever wanted to.

Heidi now stared at him with something close to curiosity.

"Oh, come on," he said. "You don't think it's just a little funny?"

"I'm too busy recovering from my shock," she said. "I don't know what is more surprising. That Lanie would ever think that one of us would want to live here, or that Ryan Harrison has a sense of humor."

He thinned his mouth. "You heard what Lanie said. We won't see some good options until September or October."

"Looks like we're stuck with each other for the summer then," Heidi said breezily, and she walked back down the path before Ryan even had a chance to respond to that, which was just as well because, like Heidi, he was left completely speechless.

5

After a long day on her feet, Heidi was looking forward to a quiet Sunday, one where she might sit out on the back deck with a glass of wine, or finish setting up her bedroom, now that she knew her time here wasn't exactly temporary.

What she wasn't looking forward to was a conversation with her mother, who was sitting on the front stoop, clearly waiting for her.

"You could have found me at the bookstore," Heidi said, knowing that her mother's reasons were clear. She wanted to scope out her daughter's living situation.

Her mother stood and gave her a quick hug. "I didn't want to bother you girls at the store, especially on a busy weekend with tourists in town. Besides, I wanted to see your new home."

Of course, she did. Heidi knew that her mother was coming from a good place, but she didn't want to have this conversation. Not now. Not ever. Besides, what was there to discuss? She'd had roommates before, they'd just never been men.

"I'd invite you in, but I'm still getting settled," she said.

Her mother's disappointment was quickly covered with a smile. "Of course. I was just passing by on the off chance that you were home."

Heidi took a steadying breath and looked at her mother frankly. "Natalie told me that she's explained the mix-up."

Her mother nodded eagerly, seeming to be relieved to finally get to the heart of her visit. "I know you've already moved in, but if you haven't even finished unpacking, then why don't I have your father come around tonight with the car? You can stay with us in the carriage house. It's cramped, but it won't be for long. Just until you find a new place."

"Thanks, Mom. But I'm good. I like it here, and this situation won't be for long, either. As soon as a new rental comes along, Ryan is moving out."

Because she sure as heck wasn't.

Still, her mother didn't look convinced. Worry drained her cheeks of their usual rosiness. "Just think about it…"

She'd thought about it, all right. She just needed her family to respect that she knew what she was doing.

"I could use your help, actually," she said, watching as her mother's mouth curved into an eager smile. "You're an expert gardener and I'm such a brown thumb. Maybe one of these days you could come over and give me some tips about gardening? I'd love to keep these shrubs blooming. Seeing as it's my home now."

Was it just her, or did her mother's teeth seem to graze in her smile?

"Sure, honey. We'll arrange a time. I'd love to help you. And see inside, of course."

"Thanks, Mom." Heidi gave her mother another quick hug and hurried inside, nearly shrieking at the sight of a man standing in the middle of her living room, even though she had hardly forgotten that Ryan was living there, thanks to that most unsuitable apartment they'd looked at yesterday.

She closed the door behind her and glanced over at his full frame. He wore dark jeans, a button-down blue shirt, and a scowl.

"Hello to you, too," she said sarcastically. "Excuse me for jumping, but this is the first time all week you've been here when I got home. Did you see my mother outside?"

"She didn't knock, so I figured she was waiting for you," Ryan said. "Besides, I didn't really know what to say to her."

Fair enough. Heidi started to kick off her shoes, pausing when she saw the frown on Ryan's face.

"If we're going to be living together, we need to establish some ground rules."

Heidi sighed. She had spent hours strategizing with Bella about how they might rearrange some of the books to give customers a new experience when they came into the shop. Like everything with Bella, it was a struggle. Her sister was set in her ways, anxious about change, even though she usually ended up taking Heidi's suggestions.

Honestly, if it was Bella's mission to drive her to other places of business, then she was succeeding. Almost.

Heidi had thought about the conversation with her sisters the entire walk home—the one both before and after the disastrous showing with Lanie. She had some good experience on her resume now. Some of the jobs that had only lasted a day (or less), she'd omitted. And Bella had written her a beautiful letter of recommendation, citing how Heidi had helped grow her business with her innovative ideas and smart approach.

But Bella was her sister. And when it came to walking into other businesses, even with familiar faces, she couldn't help but waver. She had a reputation. Even Mrs. DiStephano at the real estate office was aware of it.

Now, seeing the tight look on Ryan's face, she was reminded of that.

"Ground rules? I'm not twelve." She curled her lip and dumped her bag on the nearest chair while she kicked off her other shoe.

"Case in point." He pointed a finger of accusation at her tote bag. "There's a closet right there, with hooks. Perfect for your bag. There's ample space for your shoes, too."

She hooded her gaze and crossed her arms. She'd be damned if she did what he said, even though she'd had every intention of doing so. In her own time.

"May I lock the door first?" She shook her head, muttering a few choice words under her breath.

Ryan's gaze was sharp when she looked over at him. "Did you just call me uptight?"

"Yes," she said, not realizing that he had heard that, not that there was anything to hide. "I'm paying half my rent. I don't need to be told how to live in my own home."

He hesitated for a moment. "Fair enough."

Surprised, she picked up her bag. "Look. I know how much you like neat and order."

He frowned at that. "But you hardly know me."

She laughed as she opened the closet door, at what he'd said and at the fact that the closet was now arranged by

color and season, and divided perfectly in half. Ryan's belongings were all neatly pushed to the left, and he'd made sure to leave the entire right side for her.

The better side, she couldn't help but notice. The side with the hooks.

Deciding that it was practical, because everything about Ryan was, and nothing more than that, she set her handbag straps on one of the hooks and picked up her sandals, then tossed them onto the closet floor. She could practically feel the daggers on her back. Swallowing her pride, she bent down and set them up straight, side by side, even if they were in reversed order.

"Better?"

"Thank you," he said, looking a little sheepish.

Oh, she hadn't done this for him. No, she'd done this for herself. For her pride. And because contrary to popular belief, she did have her own system, even if it was slightly unconventional.

"Though you might find this difficult to believe, I, too, like neat and order." She just tended to do it all on big cleaning days, and not as frequently as she probably should.

She moved into the living space and flopped down on the couch. She saw Ryan wince when she went to set her feet on the coffee table, so she hovered them just above the wood surface, pretended to do a few stretches, and then lowered them slowly to the ground again.

Was it just her or did he exhale rather deeply?

"I didn't say otherwise."

She looked at him archly. "No? Your expression says otherwise."

He tried without success to lighten his features. "It's not a big ask."

No, but she suspected he had other things in mind.

"Shoes and bags in the closet. Yes, sir." She saluted him, and oh, that really pulled a scowl from his face. "Anything else I need to know while sharing our living quarters?"

He hesitated, clearly sensing that she was making fun of him. Was it the smile on her face? She was genuinely curious about what he might say next. So far, she'd considered herself to be a good roommate. Quiet, out of sight, thanks to their different schedules, and moderately neat. Had she left a spoon or two in the sink? Probably. And she was taking up more shelves in the medicine cabinet, but only because he'd already arranged his things on one shelf.

"While you're thinking of some, I have a few requests of my own." Catching the raise of his eyebrows, she grinned. "Fair's fair."

"Okay, then." He looked almost amused at the idea that he couldn't be anything less than perfect.

She stifled an eye roll as he waited, and then realized that she hadn't come up with anything yet. Darn it. That was just the problem, wasn't it? Ryan kept this house as clean as if he never lived here. Cleaner, really, considering she'd seen the way he'd folded up the throw blanket and set it back in the basket when she'd been too tired to do so, and that he'd put her spoons in the dishwasher, too. The bathroom never showed any sign of him, other than for the set of blue towels he kept in their place. His belongings were sparse and kept on the top shelf of the medicine cabinet. Courteous, perhaps. Or maybe again he was just

being practical, given that his six-foot frame made it easier for him to reach that shelf and leave her the bottom two. And it was common knowledge that women tended to have infinitely more products, which she did.

Which she didn't exactly organize very well.

"I like coffee," she said. "And sometimes I'm awakened to the smell of it, only to find that when I come into the kitchen, you've already consumed what was there and then left for the day."

"I like to clean up after myself," he said. "I would think you'd be happy I didn't leave a mess."

"I would be happier with a cup of hot coffee."

"Maybe you should get up earlier," he said with a sudden glimmer in his eyes.

She was momentarily silenced. "I'm never late for work." Not this one, at least. She sat up a little straighter on the couch, leaning in his direction as she curled her legs up under her. "How about this? On the days I get up earlier, I'll make a full pot and leave it on the burner. The days you get up, you can do the same."

"I like fresh coffee." Ryan was staring at her. "So long as you don't mind it stale, that's fine by me. I'm up at six each day. Every day," he added.

"I suppose I could get up a little earlier if I knew that I had something to look forward to," she said with a little sniff.

Ryan could only shake his head as he walked to the door. "I'll be sure to make extra tomorrow then."

"You going back to the pub?" she asked, strangely disappointed that she'd only just gotten home and that she'd be left all on her own for the night.

"Dinner plans," he said, opening the door.

Dinner plans? Just who would be having dinner with boring and uptight old Ryan Harrison? She considered the outfit, though, a bit formal for a night out with the guys.

Shielded slightly by the curtain, she shifted on the couch to stare out the window and watch him walk down the path and toward his parked car. He wasn't going into town then, or he'd surely have walked. Was he going to Pine Falls? And if so, why?

Surely Ryan Harrison couldn't have a date? And on a Sunday night?

The only thing crazier than that was the realization that she would be sort of annoyed if he did.

*

Ryan sat across from Kyle at the dining room table that his brother had built from scratch, his stomach full of a summer pasta dish and lemon meringue pie, his spirits good, as they usually were on these nights he joined his family for dinner. Sometimes, his mother came too, but she was busy these days, helping out with some of the charities and events in town, staying occupied, which he knew from experience was still her way of mending a broken heart.

He understood. All too well.

Most of the furniture in the lakefront cottage had been hand-carved by Kyle, and everything from the floorboards to the mantle had been refurnished with a detailed eye and a skilled hand. It was impressive, beautiful even, and it was meant to be Kyle's calling. He was creative and passionate, and he'd toiled away for six long years in a bar instead. Six

years when he could have been in New York, with his new wife.

Kyle's choice—or lack thereof—had almost cost him his marriage.

And even though he was reunited with Brooke, with a baby on the way, when Ryan thought of his part in it all, he still didn't know how to reconcile things. It was a guilt that he couldn't shake, no matter how much he tried and no matter how much Kyle had never thrown it in his face. And it wasn't the only one.

Growing up, Ryan had resented this side of his brother. The ability to dream while he felt compelled to keep his head down. The way he could so easily impress their father in ways that Ryan struggled.

It was only years later, long after their father's passing, that Ryan wondered if he'd ever find a way to make his father proud. Even if it was only his memory.

"How's the nursery coming along?" he asked as Brooke refilled their wine and then her water glass.

"It will be easier to finish it once we know the gender," she said with a wink across the table.

"Do you know?" Ryan stared from his brother to Brooke, wondering if he was crossing a line, but then figuring that he was already in on the secret. Maybe they'd be eager to share.

"We haven't found out yet," Kyle told him. "We're going to have a reveal party at some point soon. People do all sorts of things now to share the news. Sometimes they cut a cake, and inside it's either pink or blue. Other times they pop balloons, and see what color confetti comes out."

He slid a loving glance at Brooke, and Ryan felt his back stiffen. It had been over a year since he'd left Cleveland. Over a year since his heart had been broken. And he still didn't find it any easier to see other people exchange affection so easily when he'd struggled to hold on to a relationship, and a person, who had ended up being all wrong for him.

Even when she'd felt so right for so long.

"Well, you're welcome to hold the party at the pub," Ryan half-joked, and now Brooke excused herself from the table. Good timing, Ryan supposed.

"You thinking of creating that party room?" Kyle sipped his wine, leaning back in his chair, looking genuinely interested in what Ryan had to share.

It was a relief to have reached this point. When Ryan had first moved back to town and expressed an interest in the family business, Kyle had been defensive of the choices he'd made in keeping things the same, even offended.

They'd come a long way since then, but Ryan was still uneasy.

"I've decided to use the extra space from the back office for a lounge area instead. Get a fireplace installed. Put in some comfortable seating." That was the idea, at least. Right now everything was still covered in dust, a work in progress.

"Sounds inviting," Kyle said.

"I hope so. The changes I've made so far seemed big at first, but the result is still the same."

At first, there had been some renewed interest in the pub, people giving it a try for a drink, but that was mostly

friends and family. Until something bigger happened, and until the reputation changed, it would be difficult to attract tourists and probably more difficult to pull in locals who hadn't given the place a glance in years, if ever.

"You cleaned the joint up." Kyle's expression belayed his appreciation. "You took a few risks for the better, and last I checked, you didn't turn away business in the process."

"No, but I haven't exactly gained as much business as I'd hoped either." Ryan's sigh was as heavy as the burden on his shoulders. A year ago, it would have been his pride that took a hit that things weren't working out as well as he'd hoped. Now, it was something else. Something deeper.

"I don't think I gave you enough credit for keeping the place going as long as you did. It's not an easy job."

Kyle gave a modest shrug. "I just turned on the lights and poured the drinks. But you have a vision for the place. One that keeps things true to what Dad wanted for it, too."

Ryan nodded slowly. If he could pull it off. But a stone hearth and better music and expensive lighting didn't matter if no one wanted to give it a try.

He decided not to panic just yet. He'd panic if things were still the same three months from now.

"I still can't believe you actually run the pub." Kyle's mouth pulled into a slow grin and soon, he had tossed his head back and was laughing. "But then, your name is carved into the bar."

Ryan frowned. "What are you talking about?"

"You don't remember?" Kyle leaned forward, seeming

excited at a memory that Ryan couldn't form. "You were probably eleven, twelve. I was about seven or eight. I had gotten that wood-carving kit for Christmas, and we were spending the day after the holiday in the pub with Dad."

"Like always." Ryan felt a pang, suddenly wishing for those days, even if at the time he hadn't enjoyed it much.

"I got out my tools and I started carving my name into the wood. You did too, after a little reluctance."

Ryan tried to bring up some hint of the memory but it wasn't there. He'd buried a lot of those days, out of guilt, he supposed.

"We waited for weeks to see if Dad would say something."

"He never did," Ryan realized in surprise.

Kyle shook his head, still smiling, wistfully now. "No. He never did."

"I'm sure he knew the names were there," Ryan said.

"Oh, I'm sure." Kyle's grin was fond. "Probably liked having it there. Made him feel like we were connected to the place. Made him remember why it was important to keep it going. Made me feel that way, at least. Not that I ever planned on running the place."

Ryan felt his own grin pale in comparison, knowing how much Kyle had wished he'd done so sooner, how much it had cost his brother. "Life is a strange road. Can't say I ever planned on this either. On a lot of things, actually."

Kyle's brow lifted. "Like living with Heidi Clark?"

"How'd—" But of course. Brooke was Heidi's cousin. They all knew by now. The entire town no doubt knew.

"Brooke made me promise not to talk about it during dinner, but now that she's left the table, I figure I'm safe. So, how's that situation going?" Kyle couldn't hide his amusement.

Ryan didn't exactly blame him.

"Weird. Fine. Not so strange, actually." Ryan shrugged and reached for his wineglass. "She's rarely home at the same time as me. Works in her sister's bookshop, right?"

Kyle nodded. "Lots of businesses are all in the family around here."

True, but Heidi was the spoiled kind of girl who always had someone taking care of her. And if she thought Ryan was going to play that part when it came to her dirty spoons in the sink much longer, she'd be sorely mistaken.

"So, no…funny business going on?"

Ryan snapped his gaze to his brother and swatted at him from across the table. "What? No. She's Brooke's cousin."

"So?"

"And she's a kid," Ryan said.

"Not really," Kyle said through a sip of wine.

Ryan drained the dregs of his glass as an image of Heidi pulling those long legs up under her on the couch filled his mind. No. Not really at all.

*

Heidi tossed and turned and finally admitted to herself somewhere after midnight that she wasn't going to be able to fall asleep anytime soon. She knew what Bella would say—to turn on the light and read a book. But Heidi's contribution to the bookstore wasn't on account of her literary merit. No, she had ideas, ones that she enjoyed putting into action, but ones that she wasn't quite ready to take somewhere else.

Was that what was keeping her mind so busy? Heidi wasn't a stranger to stress, and usually, she prided herself on handling it well. What some people took as a lack of caring, Heidi called a preservation of energy. What was the sense of worrying about things that were out of your control? It was as silly as dwelling on yesterday when tomorrow was right in front of you.

And really, that was also why it was quite silly that she'd given more than a passing thought to where Ryan might have gone tonight, and with whom, just like it was very pointless of her to note the time on her phone when she heard him finally come home.

Flinging off the covers, Heidi grabbed her favorite oversized cardigan from the desk chair where she'd left it, having spent the larger portion of her night working on her resume in the quiet house, and shuffled down the hall. She was just about to round the turn into the kitchen when a light sprung on and she jumped back in surprise.

Her heart hammered against her palm as she stared at Ryan, who didn't look exactly pleased to see her either, and was probably just as surprised.

Still, her shock was momentarily abated as she let her gaze fall over the length of him. His dark hair was disheveled, and he wore glasses in a brown tortoise frame that was strangely appealing, in a book smart, nerdy sort of way. He wore pajama pants in a dusk blue plaid and a tee shirt that made her question if his shoulders had always been so defined.

Aware that she was staring, she hurried to the cabinet and grabbed a glass, then flicked on the tap, waiting for the water to run cool. Her cheeks felt flush and she wondered if the air-conditioning had gone out.

"I hope I didn't wake you," Ryan said, holding his own water glass.

"What? No." Heidi glanced over her shoulder, unnerved by the flutter that swept through her stomach again at the sight of him, and turned back to the sink to test the water temperature. She filled her glass and took a large gulp. "I couldn't sleep."

"That makes two of us then." Ryan's grin was sheepish. "What's on your mind?"

Heidi's mind went blank for the first time all night. She stared at him, deciding she quite liked the glasses and the way they accented his strong nose, and then shook her head clear.

"Work, I guess. Next steps. Lots of things that are probably so boring if I talked about them I'd manage to make myself tired again."

"Did things not work out at the bookstore?"

Maybe it was an innocent question, but it fired her up nonetheless. "Quite the opposite. It's going really well. I just have to decide where it's headed, is all." She let out a breath. She was overreacting, but he'd hit a nerve. "Ah, there, I'm feeling more tired already."

His smile seemed to come easier this time. "Wish I could say the same. I think if I started talking about all the things that are stressing me out these days, I wouldn't sleep again for a week. Maybe a month."

She waited to see if he'd elaborate and decided not to pry just yet. Ryan was someone she both knew and didn't know all at the same time. Now, though, she was curious about what his life was really like.

"Girl problems?" she wagered a guess, based on his disappearance tonight, and his attire.

His brows shot up in surprise. "No. Not anymore, at least." The way he said it made it sound like that topic was completely shut down, even preposterous.

"Bad breakup?" Why did her tone sound so hopeful? Correcting herself, she added, "I figured you had a date tonight."

"Then you're half right." Ryan set the glass on the counter, then, before she could raise an eyebrow, quickly opened the dishwasher and set it on the top rack. "I had a bad breakup before I moved back to Blue Harbor last year. As for tonight, I was at my brother's house. They invite me weekly for dinner. I think I'm becoming their charity case."

Heidi felt her chest swell as she smiled up at him. "And here I thought I was the only one with doting siblings. Gets old sometimes, but it's also nice to know that someone cares."

"True. Guess I feel like I should pay back the favor."

Heidi brightened. "Have them to my dinner party!"

Uh-oh. As soon as it was out, she realized her error. This wasn't just her home, it was a shared space, and she'd probably been presumptuous in announcing that she was planning to throw a party.

"Dinner party?" The little pinch between his eyebrows returned. "Were you ever going to mention this?"

"I'm mentioning it now," she said breezily. "I haven't set a date yet. I thought I'd check with you first." Smooth recovery, she thought, mentally patting herself on the back. She studied his expression before continuing. "It was something I thought of doing when I first signed the lease on this place. There's plenty of space to have a few people over. I thought…" She'd thought a lot of things, of course, like how this would finally get her sisters off her back, make her cousins look at her as an equal, not as the town screwup.

But no need to mention that.

"Sounds like a fun idea. And seeing how we're both related to Brooke, I'm sure my brother would love to come. Just tell me when and where." He grinned. "I mean, when."

"I'll check my calendar and get in touch with you," she said, realizing that was one of the lines she usually used after a date, though admittedly she hadn't had one in a while.

Ryan checked the clock on the range and looked momentarily put out. "I guess I should try to get some sleep if I'm going to be any use at work tomorrow. Big day, too. We've got some construction going on…"

Hence the reason for his insomnia, perhaps? Heidi opened the freezer and pulled out one of her pints of ice cream, not even bothering to check the flavor first. Glancing at it now, she was pleased with her luck.

"I'll let you in on a little secret," she said, opening a drawer to grab a spoon, and then, after a moment of hesitation, a second one. "Ice cream always does the trick. It soothes the soul. Melts the troubles away."

He grinned easier. "You sound like a commercial. Marketing background?"

Heidi's pulse skipped a beat as she slowly peeled the lid back. Was her sister being less biased than she gave her credit for? Was she actually good at this type of thing? Maybe, but convincing other business owners of that would be a challenge.

"Not exactly." She held out a spoon, and Ryan's gaze flickered in surprise.

"You're not expecting me to eat straight from that container, are you?" His expression was a combination of wonder, horror, and disgust.

She laughed. "It tastes better this way."

He gave her a knowing look. "Please. It tastes the same as in a bowl or a mug. And cleaner, too."

She pursed her lips. Of course, he'd say that. Because he was no fun. The type of guy who sat out every dance at a wedding, opting to stay safely on the sidelines, alone at a table, watching everyone else make fools of themselves. The type of guy who probably counted how many seconds he brushed his teeth, and scheduled his next dental appointment as he was walking out of his last.

The type of a guy who probably balanced his checkbook, or at least knew how much money was in his account, down to the penny.

Not that those were terrible qualities. Not at all, really.

But she wasn't letting him off the hook that easily. There was another look in his eyes. Longing, she realized. The look of someone who maybe wished they could get off their chair at a wedding, bounce around with everyone else, and have a good laugh at their own expense.

"Trust me." She held the carton out to him, one that

already bore the dent of her first spoonful. "Try it. It won't hurt you. And you might discover that you like it."

His gaze lifted from the ice cream, locking with hers instead, and something in her stomach rolled over at the exchange. Alone in a kitchen, only the sound of the air-conditioning unit humming in the background.

She was just about to pull the container back and flee the room when he reached out his hand, took the pint from her, and dug his spoon into the chocolate fudge ice cream. He took a bite, savoring it, his gaze narrowing as if he was appraising the situation.

She waited for him to be the mood killer he usually was. To put a dose of reality on one of her favorite guilty pleasures.

Just as quickly as he'd taken the pint, he handed it back to her. He then carefully opened the dishwasher and set his spoon inside.

"You're right," he said. "It does taste better. And…I feel a little better too."

"Let me guess," Heidi teased. "You have to brush your teeth again now."

His brow shot up. "Of course!" But he was grinning as walked out of the kitchen.

Heidi's own smile still lingered when she heard the door to his bedroom close a few minutes later. She leaned back against the counter and dug her spoon back into the ice cream, feeling the cold chocolate melt down her throat as she replayed the last few minutes.

She felt better too. And something told her it wasn't just because of the dessert in her hand.

6

The prettiest shop in all of Blue Harbor was, of course, Something Blue. It was also, perhaps, the most coveted place to shop, and not only because of the ever-changing gorgeous window displays of custom-made wedding gowns or the flutes of champagne that Brooke promised her customers. The bridal shop seemed to glisten and sparkle in a way that made even the most reluctant hearts think about a walk down the aisle.

Heidi could only grin. Of all the shops in town that she was considering pitching her services to, Something Blue still hadn't made her list. Brooke had created a fantasy here, capturing every detail that touched on the deepest of emotions. From the velvet seating to the soft music to chandeliers, Something Blue wasn't really a shop; it was an experience.

And one that Heidi could learn a lot from.

Heidi paused outside the storefront and gazed at the lace gown in the window, noticing how the skirt gathered at the bottom in an elegant pool of silky fabric. She wasn't one of those women who planned her wedding, or even fantasized about it much, but standing here, taking in this dress, she could start to understand all the hype.

The door to the shop opened, pulling Heidi from her

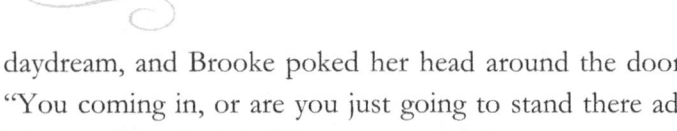

daydream, and Brooke poked her head around the door. "You coming in, or are you just going to stand there admiring my work all day?"

Heidi laughed. "I could certainly admire your work all day. And that's exactly why I'm coming inside." That and the fact that while the Firefly Café may be closed on Mondays, the bookstore was not, and she was pressed for time.

She followed her cousin into the storefront, where her sister Bella and their cousins—and their cousins—were already gathered, some flipping through Brooke's lookbook on the coffee table in the seating area, others carefully going through the dressers on hangers.

Everything in the shop was made personally by Brooke, and while most of it was designed specifically for each client, she also liked to keep a healthy inventory of dresses that brides could buy off the rack.

Today, Amelia Conway was the bride in question. She was marrying her high school sweetheart, after many years apart. Across the room, Heidi watched her shake her head when her sister Cora pointed to a satin ballgown. No, that wouldn't be Amelia's taste. Amelia would want something more simple.

The ballgown was more her cousin Gabby's style. Heidi almost laughed when she saw that Gabby was already wearing one of the veils, even though she was not yet engaged, though probably would be soon.

"Champagne?" Brooke held out a flute to her, and Heidi took it gratefully.

The only one not drinking was Brooke, but then, she was technically working, which made it an easy excuse, even though she was family and the other ladies wouldn't mind if she joined them. Heidi noticed the glow on her cousin's face and bit back a smile, wondering when she'd choose to share the exciting news with everyone.

But today was Amelia's day. The day she would be choosing her wedding gown, with all of their input, of course.

"You know me. I'm not fussy," Amelia was heard saying to her sister Maddie, who was trying to encourage her to try on a frothy tulle creation, something straight out of a fairytale.

"And remember," Brooke said, turning to address the woman of the hour. "If you don't find something you like, tell me what you do and don't like about these options. I'll design you the perfect gown in time for your big day."

"Whenever that is," Britt commented, giving her sister a questioning look.

Amelia gave a little smile. "End of August. We finally decided on a date."

End of August. And it was already nearly July. It seemed so soon yet so far away when Heidi considered her living arrangements.

"Well, it's about time!" Candy exclaimed as she crossed the room. Most of the women looked as startled as Heidi felt.

"I didn't hear you come in," Brooke said delicately. She glanced back at the door as if checking to see if she'd remembered to close it.

"Oh, you know me. I'm so light on my feet." Candy motioned to her bright pink heels and then thundered over

to where her stepdaughters were gathered. "Amelia, I know the perfect dress for you."

Amelia looked nervously at her sister Britt and then cleared her throat. "I thought I'd have some fun trying a few on, getting a feel for what I like."

"I know *exactly* what you'll like," Candy said, pinching her lips.

Heidi exchanged a secret smile with her cousin Jenna across the room. The pressure was off the rest of them for now. When it came to weddings, Candy considered herself a person of authority, after having planned her own wedding and then Britt's so recently.

Brooke was the only person in the room who looked potentially more put out than Amelia. Though Candy's wedding to Dennis Conway had been nearly a year ago, it lived in infamy within these four walls. There had been too many redesigns and requests for changes to count, right up until the very day of the wedding.

Still wearing the veil, Gabby took a long swig of her champagne and then refilled the glass. No doubt she too was remembering Candy's ever-changing mind when it came to her flower arrangements.

Though Amelia might be the antithesis of a bridezilla, Candy was far from shy in her opinions, and as Amelia's stepmother, she would no doubt be heavily involved in the process, or expect to be, at least.

"I'd love to see you try on a few gowns," Heidi said. That was the reason they were all gathered here, after all.

Candy slid her eyes across the room, her blue gaze widening as her finger came out, wagging in Heidi's direction.

"Ah, Heidi! I was hoping I'd see you here today!"

Uh-oh. The crystal chandelier rattled a little with each of Candy's purposeful strides. Behind her, Amelia's shoulders seem to sag in relief, and she and her sisters went back to chatting about their options.

Brooke quickly slipped into the back room, and the rest of the girls seemed to scatter like birds, leaving Heidi to deal with Candy all on her own.

"I hear you're living with Ryan Harrison!"

Of course. It was bound to happen. Heidi gave a mild smile and said, "Just for the summer. Or unless something else opens up."

"In Blue Harbor? Not likely, at least not until the fall." Candy reached out and took Heidi's glass from her hand and took a long sip of the champagne. "Now, tell me. Is that man as uptight as he appears to be? Does he make his bed with hospital corners?"

"I haven't been inside his bedroom," Heidi informed her. She eyed the champagne glass, wondering how she could tactfully reach for a new one.

"No?" Candy's eyes waggled as her mouth quirked. "Not yet, at least."

Heidi let out a bark of laughter. "Please. Ryan Harrison? The man must be what…forty?"

"Thirty-six, last I checked," Candy said with a wink. "And handsome. Single, too."

"And uptight," Heidi reminded her. Rather boring, no fun at all.

Candy, however, seemed to tap into the reservations that Heidi harbored. "Oh, I don't know about that," she

said lightly. "I think he just needs the right girl to come along and shake him out of his shell."

She handed back Heidi's now empty glass and hurried off to the dressing rooms to start giving her opinions on something else for a few precious minutes.

Heidi used the opportunity to walk over to her sister, who jumped a little when she approached. Her fingers dropped the veil she'd been admiring, and her cheeks had a guilty flush to them when she turned around.

Heidi fought back a smile. It was so obvious that Bella was falling in love with Craig, and why shouldn't she be? The man was handsome and kind and shared all of her interests.

He was her perfect match. And she'd be best to remember that when it came time to think about dating again. She'd want to find a man who shared her energy and her zest for life and didn't sweat the small stuff.

The problem was that the guys she'd gone out with who had all these traits had turned out to be friends and nothing more.

"If you're worried I'm going to tease you about Craig, don't worry. Though I will say that chiffon dress you've been eyeing would look perfect on you."

"Stop." Bella gave her a playful swat, but Heidi could see that she was pleased.

"Actually, I wanted to follow up on my invitation to have you and your wonderful man to dinner one night. Would Friday or Saturday work?"

"This week?" Bella looked puzzled. "I wasn't sure you'd still be doing that. That's why I haven't come over… I mean, won't it be weird, all things considered?"

"Why should it be weird? You all know Ryan. And it's my house, too. It's no different than when I had roommates at my last place in Pine Falls." Only it was different, and she just couldn't say why. Or admit it. Even fully to herself.

"If you're sure…"

"Very sure. I'm heading to the store after this to get some ingredients," Heidi said.

"But it's only Monday," Bella said with a laugh.

"Tell that to all the people who claim I never plan ahead." Heidi gave her sister a pointed look.

"Have you thought about pitching to any shops? The salon could probably use a refresh. Nina took it over from her mother and never made many changes."

Heidi considered it. It was true that the salon was comfortable but might do with some new changes. "I'm not sure their business needs much help, though."

Bella shrugged. "You never know unless you ask."

Exactly. And that was the part of the process that Heidi couldn't face just yet. Because what if she did ask, and everyone said no? And she had no one to blame but herself?

*

If Heidi was going to have a dinner party, then she would need to practice. Really, she would need to learn how to cook, but honestly, how hard could it be? She knew the basics. She could make herself pizza, a sandwich, even an omelet, or at least a scrambled egg version of one.

Armed with the ingredients for the recipe she'd copied from one of the cookbooks at the shop, she set everything

out on the counter and read through the instructions again, thinking that a clearer definition of minced might be helpful about now.

An open-concept living space might, too. She fumbled to prop her phone against the backsplash amidst the cluttered counter, trying to keep one eye on the video tutorial and another on the knife in her hand.

She finally had the onions sauteing in a pan (at least she thought they were sauteing) when Ryan appeared in the doorway, sniffing the air with a gleam in his eye.

"Something smells good. And here I was thinking that this kitchen might not get much use."

"I'm doing a practice run for when everyone comes to dinner," Heidi said, frowning down at the cans of tomatoes and then letting her eyes drift to the breadcrumbs and chicken. "And a straightforward dish. Now I'm wondering if I could order takeout from Firefly Café and pass it off as my own."

But then, how could she still invite Amelia? Bad idea. Contrary to what Bella might say these days, not all of her thoughts were brilliant ones.

"Or grub from Harrison's," Ryan said.

He couldn't be serious. But something in his expression told her that he might be.

Heidi felt a flush of panic at the mere thought of it. She'd have to pull this dinner off because even her food would be better than the bar food they served in that pub.

"You could always grill out?"

She wrinkled her nose. "I could, but it's my first time inviting anyone to dinner and I want it to be special."

Proper. Impressive. Already her mind was filling with images of clusters of long candles, their wax dripping in intricate patterns, soft classical music, and open bottles of good wine.

Oh, who was she kidding? Certainly not herself. Maybe she should just open a bag of chips and throw some burgers on the grill.

"Want any help?" When she didn't respond right away, he added, "Don't worry, it's still going to be your dinner party. Consider me your sous chef."

"If you're sure…" In other words, she'd take all the help she could get, even if it meant putting up with Ryan telling her what to do for the next hour. If she could learn the recipe tonight, she'd have it perfected by the time everyone came to dinner.

Without wasting another minute, Ryan opened the pantry door and removed an apron from the hook.

"I assumed that the Tinleys left that behind." Heidi watched as he tied it around his waist, accentuating his lean hips and broad chest. She cleared her throat and looked back away. No sense in letting her mind drift now, not when she was holding a sharp object. "I thought you didn't cook."

"Not cooking and not knowing how to cook are two different things." He gave her a crooked smile and stepped forward, scooching close to her in the cramped space with minimal counter space. He picked up the recipe and studied it carefully before inspecting her ingredients.

Heidi braced herself, waiting for him to say something overly adult and terribly annoying. To fend him off, she

said, "Don't worry. I plan to clean up everything once I'm done."

Admittedly, the small surface was a mess. Piled with all the ingredients she'd purchased at the store after leaving the bridal salon. She must have been crazy to think she could prepare a full meal for a large group in this space. And with her family and their dates alone, it would be a large group, even if some wouldn't be able to make it.

"We can set up a breading station at the table," Ryan said. He stirred the onions and then lowered the heat on the range. "Have you minced the garlic yet?"

She fought off a smile. "You know how to mince?"

He gave her a funny look. "Um, yeah. Don't you?"

"Of course I do," she bristled. Rummaging through the piles of groceries on the two-by-three-foot space, she found the pre-minced jarred garlic and held it up triumphantly.

He shook his head, but she could tell he was amused. For a few minutes, they worked in companionable silence, him at the stove on the sauce, while she did her best to set up what he called a breading station. The recipe did not detail this, unfortunately, and she cursed herself for not helping her mother out more in the kitchen.

"So, where'd you learn to cook?" she asked.

"I used to cook a lot. Back in Cleveland," Ryan said. His back was to her as he stood at the range, and eventually, he said, "But cooking for one seems a little pointless. With my long hours it also just became easier to eat on the job. That's probably why I'm so eager to change the menu at the pub."

She laughed. That would be one reason, but she was too polite to say the other, more glaring one. Harrison's Pub was a local institution, a neighborhood watering hole, and a guy's bar. It wasn't known for its ambiance and certainly not for its food. Though, in fairness, she hadn't been in there in...years. And even then, it had only been a few times to shoot pool and have a beer.

"Brooke tells me that you've done a lot with the place in the past year," she said.

"Not enough." Ryan looked troubled when he turned to face her, and she couldn't tell if it was because of the bar or because she still wasn't quite sure what a breading station was.

Trying not to laugh, he came closer to inspect her work. Feeling like she was being approached by a judging panel, she stepped aside, trying to formulate an excuse even though she wasn't quite sure what to say.

When in doubt, honesty was probably the best policy, she decided.

"I'm afraid I'm not as experienced as you are in the kitchen," she said. "My meals are mostly takeout, dinners out, or frozen entrees. However, I make a mean grilled cheese and a killer bowl of spaghetti with jarred sauce."

He was watching her closely, his expression unreadable, but not what she was expecting. Instead of annoyance or judgment, or the typical lack of surprise, he looked very surprised, and in a good way.

"You left out ice cream. You make an awesome midnight snack."

Heidi pulled in a breath and released it slowly, struggling

to hide her smile as Ryan walked to the cabinets and found two dishes. "Crack some eggs into the one and give them a whisk." He paused long enough for her to burst out laughing.

"I do know what a whisk is. And how to use it. I forgot to mention that I also make delicious scrambled eggs."

"I'll have to try them sometime," he said, sliding her a grin.

Her heart sped up as she turned and pulled a whisk from the utensils drawer, then began cracking the eggs into the dish while Ryan seasoned the bread crumbs. She thought about what he'd said about how he used to cook. Until cooking became for one.

"So, tell me about the changes at Harrison's," she said while she whisked.

Ryan dragged out a sigh. "I cleaned the place up, I suppose. Brought in more light. Reconfigured some of the tables. Minor changes that felt major at the time. But it's no Carriage House Inn. Certainly not the Yacht Club. And it's still pulling from the usual crowd. And trust me, they liked it the way it was. I guess I feel like instead of improving the place, I've just found a way to make it worse."

Heidi's eyes popped. She didn't think it was possible for the place to be much worse unless you were one of the old widowers who lived there every afternoon, or one of the frat boys who liked watching the game and drinking shots.

"It was definitely brighter when I stopped in last week," she said, hoping to sound more positive than she felt about the place.

His eyed hooded. "Don't worry. You don't have to

tiptoe around my feelings. The place is a dump."

Heidi was about to ask why he'd taken it over then, but she knew the answer already. He was being a good brother. He had let Kyle off the hook, giving him a chance to pursue his passion for once.

But something told her that it was more than that. Maybe, this could be Ryan's passion. Because he clearly cared.

She watched as he expertly drudged the chicken through the eggs and the breadcrumbs, then transferred them to another pan on the stove.

"Should we eat at the table?" Like real adults, she thought to herself.

He hesitated and then transferred the chicken to a baking dish and began topping it with the cheese. "Oh, I don't want to intrude."

"Nonsense! You helped cook everything." More like he had cooked everything. And she'd watched.

And he was too nice a guy to point that out, even though he knew it.

The Ryan she knew would have pointed it out and then given her a judgmental look over it. Or maybe not. Maybe she really didn't know Ryan at all.

But she was starting to…and so far, she liked what she saw.

"Besides," she said, taking two plates from the cabinet. "We need to taste the food to make sure it's good enough to serve to our guests."

"Our guests, huh?"

Figure of speech, she told herself. But it did have a nice ring to it.

*

Once they were settled on the back deck, wine glasses filled, Heidi decided to get a read on the local gossip, and she knew it didn't just fly around with the women.

"So, are the guys giving you a hard time for our living situation?"

Ryan laughed. "How could they not? It's not exactly conventional."

"It's better than living in that place Lanie showed us." Heidi shuddered just thinking about it and took a bite of her food, smiling at how good it tasted. "I can't believe that she thought one of us would take it."

"She overestimated our dislike for each other, I guess." He glanced up. "Not that I dislike you."

She pursed her lips. Maybe that was the case now, but she was under no illusions that he was far from fond of her in the past. She shrugged. "And how can I dislike you when you've cooked me this delicious dinner?"

"I thought that you were supposed to be the one cooking it..." His eyes shifted as he reached for his wine.

Heidi laughed. "I thought so too. Good thing I was paying attention to what you were doing. I'll need all the help I can get come next weekend when everyone comes over."

"You look nervous," Ryan observed.

"It's silly." Heidi tried to shake off the feelings but they were still there. "My sisters are always doing things for me. I guess I want to just prove to them that I'm...equal, you could say."

"Birth order is a tough thing to shake," Ryan agreed. "In my case, I'm the oldest. I'm the serious one. The one who holds the line." He paused and looked thoughtfully into the yard as he sipped his wine. "Though most people would probably agree that Kyle's the one who has done that. Held down the pub while I was living in Cleveland, pursuing a career I thought I'd love instead of admitting that it was just a job and paycheck. Middle management."

"So you like running the pub then?" She was as surprised as anyone. Including Kyle, she knew.

"Never knew how much more meaningful it would be to have something of my own, you could say."

She nodded. "I get it." She felt her cheeks heat. There was no comparing her situation to his. He was focused. He'd held down a corporate job for years, and now he was running a family business, all on his own. "I mean, I understand the importance of doing a job that you care about."

She waited to see if he'd give her a funny look, like most people in town did when she talked about a new venture or idea in the past, but to her surprise, he didn't.

"So…you moved back just to help your brother?"

"And be close to my mother," Ryan said with a nod.

Heidi looked at him over the rim of her wineglass. There was that look again, a strange shadow in his eyes she'd seen before that told her that there was much more going on in his head than he was willing to say. And a much bigger reason why he had decided to return to Blue Harbor, give up his life's path to that point, and run a dive bar of all things.

Especially in his preppy khakis and button-down shirts. Even if they did look quite good on him.

Not that she was really paying much attention.

7

The dinner party was scheduled for seven on Saturday, but Heidi felt like she'd been working on it since noon. It would be a smaller affair than Heidi had planned because not everyone could make it. Natalie's babysitter had fallen through, and their parents had an anniversary party to attend and couldn't babysit Zoe, meaning only Bella and her boyfriend Craig would be coming from Heidi's immediate family. Kyle and Brooke would be in attendance, of course, and Lanie Thompson, the only single person in the group, other than Heidi. And Ryan.

It was a warm night and, with any luck, the breeze would stay at bay. Heidi had roped strings of lights over the back deck and Ryan had carried out extra chairs and a folding table earlier that morning, that Heidi had then covered in a tablecloth. She'd clipped the best of the flowers from the yard and now tried to arrange them in vases the way her cousin Gabby did in her store, but try as she might, they still looked unbalanced, and the leaves seemed to spread out more than they did at Sweet Stems, some of the blooms being stubbornly longer than the others, and then, upon clipping the ends, too short.

Heidi finally sighed and stepped back from the table, which was already set with place cards she'd crafted out of origami flowers—a pastime that she also put to use in the display windows at the bookstore sometimes. The deck was small, and with the tables, it would be tight, especially with the extra chairs pulled in from the kitchen, but no one would mind. The pink roses still bunched together stubbornly, and she was beginning to regret including the purple flowers she couldn't even name. For all she knew they were weeds, but they were pretty. And there wasn't time left to change anything. She had as much chance of creating a showstopping centerpiece as she did getting insight into Ryan's romantic history. The man was decidedly clammed up when it came to his personal life. Quiet. Private.

And achingly mysterious.

Right. None of that. That was Candy getting into her head, who right now was being swept away for a date night on Evening Island with her husband so there was no risk of her crashing the dinner, something she was prone to do despite being of the next generation and not on the invitation list. And the only thing that Heidi should be thinking about right now was the chicken waiting to be prepped so that all she would have to do was slide it into the oven when her guests arrived.

Thirty minutes later, with a few curse words muttered and much regret felt about choosing to get all dressed and primped before tackling the breading station, Heidi stepped back from the counter and straight into something hard. And warm.

One glance over her shoulder confirmed what she already knew. Ryan's chest was directly at her eye level.

Sliding her gaze higher, she saw the telltale sheen of amusement pass through his expression before she could step away.

"I came home as soon as I could get away. The construction went long today since they don't work tomorrow, and I needed to sign off on a few things." His voice trailed off as his gaze roved over her, then, catching her eye, he looked sharply at the platters on the counter. "Looks like you didn't need me after all."

"Oh, I wouldn't say that," Heidi said with a shy smile. "I didn't get a chance to thank you for helping me cook the other night. If I hadn't watched what you did, I don't think I'd be able to pull this off." And there was no guarantee that it would taste as good, either.

"It was nice to cook again," Ryan said. "I might even do it more often."

Heidi wondered if those plans included her. All week she'd been surprised to find that there was a cup's worth of coffee still warm in the carafe for her each morning after Ryan had already left for the day. The hours at the bookstore didn't overlap with his hours at the bar, so they'd barely seen each other since their dinner. Now, she felt a little strange thinking that they were coming together again, to welcome people into the place that they both called home at the moment.

She trusted her friends and family not to say anything. They were all one big social group. This was nothing new.

Except…it felt new. Something felt new.

She glanced away, her heart pounding at the way he was looking at her.

"I can't say that I will be cooking more often." Heidi sighed at the mess that had already accumulated on the counters and began quickly putting everything away, knowing she'd better hurry unless she wanted her guests to realize just what an effort this had been for her. "All this work and then it gets eaten within minutes!"

Ryan laughed. "Let's hope our guests appreciate it." He raised his eyebrows when the doorbell rang. "I didn't even know there was a doorbell to this house."

"I wonder who's the first to arrive? Bets?" She grinned. "I love betting."

"That doesn't surprise me," Ryan said, giving her a rueful look that made her again wonder just how much of her reputation defined her in this small town. Well, it was one she was shaking. And tonight was another opportunity.

Still, he rubbed his chin, showing that he was willing to play along. "Probably my brother. I know I say he takes life too casually, but he's surprisingly more on top of things than I ever gave him credit for."

"He surprised you then," she said.

"People can." His blue gaze seemed to linger on her long enough for her to forget that there were people standing on their doorstep, waiting. But it was summer, a warm night, and—

And nothing. She finished wiping down the small counter as quickly as her arm would move.

"My money's on Bella. She's nothing if not precise."

"Winner buys ice cream?" His grin stopped her breath when he paused in the doorway.

Heidi felt her cheeks flush when she saw the way his

eyebrows lifted at the simple question. Either way, they'd be spending more time together. Heidi didn't see how she could argue with his proposal. Or if she wanted to.

"Deal," she said. "I'll get the appetizers out if you want to do the honors."

A moment later, a triumphant Ryan appeared in the doorway of the clean enough kitchen with Brooke and Kyle.

"Something smells wonderful! Did you make that sauce yourself?" Brooke bent down to smell the pan of chicken parmesan, which would go into the oven once everyone arrived.

"I had a good teacher," Heidi said, locking eyes with Ryan.

"Ah." Brooke lifted the copy of the recipe from the counter. "I know this cookbook. One of my favorites."

"I have a lot of time to look through them in the store on slow days," Heidi said. Then, remembering her manners, she asked, "Wine?"

She pulled a bottle of wine (Conway blend, of course) from the fridge and took three glasses from the cabinet. Then, realizing her error, she grabbed a fourth. She watched Ryan's shoulders visibly sag with relief.

"Oh, none for me," Brooke said casually. "Early morning tomorrow. I'm meeting with Amelia to go over her designs for the dress. I only pray that Candy won't catch wind of it and join us. It's one of the reasons that Britt asked their dad to take Candy to the island for an overnight stay. We're hoping Candy's reluctant to leave before the brunch buffet."

Heidi laughed as she filled everyone's glasses and poured Brooke a lemonade. "Ah, so they're staying at Natalie's hotel. Too bad she isn't working tomorrow or she could have been your spy. But I don't think you have anything to worry about. No guest would check out without indulging in that buffet."

"Too bad Amelia can't join us tonight," Brooke continued. "But I think she's gotten more used to having Candy's help at the restaurant than she lets on."

"The Firefly Café is always packed," Heidi said, and then, seeing the glance that passed between Ryan and Kyle, realized her error. It was the reason why Jackson Bradford wouldn't be coming over for dinner either, though he did promise to try to stop by if he had the chance. It was a Friday night, in summer, in Blue Harbor. Most of the restaurants had a line ten people deep.

And then there was Harrison's…

Saved by the sound of the doorbell ringing again, Heidi set down her wineglass and hurried to the door. Sure enough, Bella and Craig stood on the stoop bearing a bottle of wine and a bouquet of flowers, and coming up behind them were Lanie and Jenna—her boyfriend was busy with his grandmother tonight, leaving the two women to fill out the table on their own, which Heidi found to be quite a relief because sitting with Ryan and three other couples would have been stranger than their living arrangements already were.

And that left the last of the couples. Maddie and Cole called out from the sidewalk as they hurried up to the front stoop. Cora and Britt had been invited but had other plans, which was just as well, given the size of the cottage. Gabby, of course, had a wedding to attend. No season was bigger than summer for her flower shop, and she usually stayed for the reception as an honorary guest.

"I brought dessert as promised," Maddie said, proffering a white bakery box that smelled of rich, dark chocolate.

"Thank you," Heidi said gratefully. She smiled up at Cole. "Everyone's on the back deck."

She led them into the kitchen and set the bakery box on the counter. The screen door was open and the music was playing just loud enough not to overshadow the lively buzz that was already filling the yard. Remembering the citronella candles she'd stocked up on, Heidi grabbed the lighter and followed the last of her guests outside, tending to each flame.

She looked around at everyone sipping wine or beer, enjoying the appetizers she'd made (or at least semi-made if one might count adding fresh avocado to store-bought guacamole homemade) and saw Ryan approaching her with two wineglasses.

"Figured you might need this," he whispered to her, handing her a glass.

She gave a little smile and then felt her cheeks heat when she saw Maddie watching her from across the small crowd with a suspicious look on her face. Something told her that there would be some explaining to do before the night was over. Not that she could explain what was happening between her and Ryan to anyone…including to herself.

*

Ryan watched from across the deck as Heidi did what she did best. She laughed at Cole's jokes, she leaned in to hear what Maddie had to say, she changed the music when the songs got stale, and she served her dinner with a flourish.

Ryan didn't have the heart to tell her that she'd forgotten the garlic, or that the onions were burnt, and the chicken was overcooked. Neither did anyone else. And really, no one cared.

Dusk had settled in and the strings of lights and glow from the candles gave a festive feeling to the otherwise simple space. Conversation and laughter seemed to echo against the chirping of crickets, something that he hadn't experienced in his own home since he'd come back to Blue Harbor, and even then, his life in Cleveland had been quiet. His girlfriend of four years had been like him, preferring to keep their dinners to the two of them, a few times a year maybe adding another couple to the mix. The conversation was polite and easy, and at the time it had seemed like enough,

Now, Ryan wondered how long it had been since he'd ever let himself laugh like this. Let himself sit back and have an extra glass of wine, and not care if his food was overdone and underseasoned.

"I'm just glad that we weren't too late," Maddie said. She gave Ryan a disapproving look, but there was a shine to her eyes. "Cole tells me you're a real workhorse."

Ryan took the joke and held up a hand by a way of apology. "I'd be lying if I said I didn't want the renovation done yesterday, but Cole and his team are ahead of schedule."

Maddie looked at her boyfriend with pride. "Well, you won't find a better contractor around. You've seen what he's done at the bakery."

Ryan had, and it was the reason he'd hired the man. They hadn't been friends back in school—Cole had been a troubled kid, and he'd gotten into trouble too—but time had minimized their differences. They weren't the same people they'd been back then.

He glanced at Heidi. Maybe she wasn't the same either. Or maybe, she was exactly who she'd always been and he'd misjudged her.

He caught Cole's humble grin across the table. Misjudged a lot of people.

"Well, we'll all have to come in once it's finished and celebrate you both," Jenna said. "And you, too, Kyle."

"Oh, no," Kyle said, holding up his hands. "My days at the pub are over. It's all in Ryan's hands now."

Across the table, he grinned, but Ryan struggled to swallow his chicken, and not just because it was chewy.

"This is delicious," Bella said and raised a glass. "To the hostess."

Heidi's cheeks turned pink from across the table, but it was clear that she was pleased. "I can't take all the credit. Ryan taught me this recipe."

Oh, jeez. This was one recipe he'd rather not take credit for, but still, he shared a smile across the table and held up a hand. "I'm just a guest tonight."

"To Heidi," Lanie said, lifting her glass. "And Ryan. Who would have known that such a mix-up could result in such a fun night?"

Who indeed?

"Speaking of fun nights, we'll all have to do something for Heidi's thirtieth birthday. It's just around the corner," Maddie suggested.

"I'm practically middle-aged," Heidi said dramatically.

"Anything planned yet?" Kyle asked, posing the exact question Ryan was thinking.

"I haven't even made it all the way through tonight," Heidi said with a laugh. "At least let me get through this and then I can start thinking about the next party."

"If it's anything like this one, you can count me in," Brooke said. "I love how you've set up this backyard. Gives me ideas for our place, though I'm not sure why I never thought about putting up strings of light before."

"I agree. And at least we know that, if things don't work out at the bookstore, you have other skills," Bella said.

Ryan wondered if the rest of the group noticed the shadow that fell over Heidi's face, even though it was soon replaced with a bright smile.

"Not that I ever doubted you," Bella said quickly, looking alarmed. "Besides, Heidi is very aware that I think she should be pursuing opportunities beyond my humble establishment."

Heidi rolled her eyes dramatically and said to the table, "I think my sister is trying to fire me. What do you all think?"

They all laughed, but Bella was shaking her head. "I mean it. Heidi has real talent. She's completely turned my store around and I didn't even know it needed help."

Brooke nodded. "Your new window display is

incredible. I love all the paper beach umbrellas and the sand. Was that your work, Heidi?"

Heidi grumbled something under her breath and picked up her wineglass. She seemed to hide behind it as she took a slow sip.

Ryan narrowed his eyes on her, finding this surprising, and maybe a little telling. The girl he'd always known was the version he'd seen earlier in the evening. Loud, fun, warm, and confident. This girl was different. Someone was paying her a compliment, and she didn't want to take it.

He couldn't understand why.

"It was just a window display," she finally said, brushing her hand through the air.

"It was more than that," Craig cut in. "And that sand was swiped straight from the public beach, not that anyone better let Mayor Hudson find out!"

Ryan laughed along with everyone else. He realized with a sense of shame that not long ago, he might have found that more sophomoric than inspiring.

"And I'm a newcomer here so I can give my opinion with less bias than all of you," Craig continued. "Heidi's also come up with new ideas for how to display the merchandise in the store. I'm just hoping she'll stick around by the time my next release is out."

Ryan hadn't read any of Craig's books, but for how famous he was, he didn't show it. He was a good fit for this town. And for the Clark and Conway family, Ryan thought.

Glancing at his brother, also part of the family now, Ryan again felt that pressing unease. It was a group he wouldn't mind belonging to either, permanently.

"People are buying things in my store that they used to walk by in the past," Bella nodded. "I think I was too close to it to recognize areas for improvement, but Heidi brought a fresh perspective to my business. I couldn't be more impressed."

Neither, Ryan realized, could he.

"Please." Heidi's cheeks looked ruddy and she rearranged her utensils on the table. "You're my sister, so you have to say that."

"I don't," Craig said, grinning.

Heidi threw him a rueful look, and then abruptly stood up. "Who else is ready for dessert? Maybe with coffee, in the living room?" She glanced at Ryan and he nodded, pleased to be included in the decision.

"Oh," Brooke cut in. "Before we leave the table, there's something that Kyle and I wanted to share with everyone."

Heidi's eyes darted to Ryan's, and his, in turn, darted to Kyle, wondering if he'd caught that exchange. Fortunately, his eyes were only on his wife.

"Of course!" Heidi sat back down again, seeming pleased.

Brooke reached over and took Kyle's hand, giving him one of those loving gazes that made something in Ryan's gut twist. He knew they were happy, but he still couldn't shake the feeling that he'd played a part in their separation all those years ago. There were some things that words weren't enough to apologize for, which was why he'd need to show him. And he was trying every day.

"We told my sisters and parents last night, and well, Ryan already knows, too, so while we're all together

tonight, we thought it would be the perfect time to tell you that we're going to soon be a family of three!"

A whoop of delight went up from the table and all the women were immediately on their feet, hurrying around the table to give Brooke a hug, who laughed at their reactions while Kyle shook the hands of the men, accepting their congratulations with a look of both pride and apprehension.

Ryan watched to see how Heidi would react, relieved to see that she played along as if she had just heard the news for the first time.

"No wonder you haven't had a sip of wine all night!" she said to Brooke, giving him a wink across the room.

It wasn't until they were in the kitchen, him getting a pot of coffee brewing and her plating the chocolate tarts that Maddie had brought, that she turned to him and said, "I guess I can't blackmail you anymore now, huh?" Her mouth curved into a grin that put a smile on his own face.

"I guess that will make it easier for me to stay here at the house."

"Oh, come on now, you didn't really think I'd kick you out?" She gave a little shrug. "Besides, you've started to grow on me."

"Oh yeah?" His chest warmed at her words because he realized that she was starting to grow on him too, and that whenever this strange arrangement of theirs ended, he might not be as relieved as he'd once thought he'd be.

8

Heidi was awakened by the smell of brewing coffee, inviting her to toss back the covers and throw on an old cardigan, even though it was earlier than her usual wake-up time, especially for a Sunday and her day off from the bookstore.

She padded down the hall, wiping the sleep from her eyes, and halted in the kitchen when she saw Ryan sitting at the table in the small nook, reading over some paperwork, a coffee mug in hand.

"I made enough for you, as promised," he said, gesturing to the pot on the counter. "But I'll warn you this is my third cup."

"Too much wine last night?" Heidi darted her eyes from his faded blue tee shirt and grey sweatpants, thinking the look was strangely casual for a man who was usually so formal.

"Just...another night of bad sleep."

Heidi nodded in understanding as she filled her favorite mug (it was Christmas-themed, and a gift from Cora Conway, who owned the holiday shop in town where Natalie worked during the winter months, but it was the perfect size for her morning brew any day of the year) and opened the fridge in search of milk. She was pleased to see the

leftover tarts from Buttercream Bakery sitting in a plastic container on the top shelf.

She pulled it out now, along with the milk, and plated her unconventional breakfast. Then, after a brief hesitation, she added a second tart and grabbed two forks from the drawer. After she'd made her coffee to her liking with extra milk and sugar, she carried everything to the table, hoping that she wasn't intruding, but deciding it would be strange to go into the living room like she might have done if she'd been alone this morning.

"There's no better way to start your day than with some chocolate," she said, gesturing to the plate.

"Here I thought it was with coffee," Ryan said, setting down his paperwork.

She could tell from a quick glance that they were financial papers, much like the ones she'd seen her sister poring over a couple of months ago with a worried pinch in her forehead that she couldn't hide no matter how hard she tried. Luckily, those days were over. Revenues were up, thanks to a few new marketing efforts and pricing changes, but Heidi knew better than to take credit for it. It was Bella's store, and one that she'd built with love and care.

Making sense of numbers had never been Heidi's strength, so she wasn't in a position to offer her opinion, but from the wariness she saw in Ryan's eyes behind his smudged glasses, she felt the need to do something.

"Here," she said, leaning across the table.

Ryan frowned in response as her hands closed the distance between them. "What are you doing?" he asked nervously, visibly stiffening.

She couldn't help but laugh under her breath. The man was wound so tight, that it would take more than those two glasses of wine last night to calm him down a bit.

"Just...trust me," she said, giving him a shake of the head. "I'm not going to hurt you."

Carefully, she lifted the glasses from his face, noticing how the blueness of his eyes brightened when they weren't hiding behind the lenses.

"They're all smudged," she said in a slightly scolding tone, then wiped them down with the edge of her soft sweater until they were clear.

"There. Isn't that a better way to start the day?" She gave him a knowing smile as she handed over the glasses.

Ryan slowly put them back on his face and gave her a hint of a smile. "Certainly a clearer one."

Something seemed to pass through his gaze that made her wonder if he was talking about more than just his vision. After a few moments of silence spent sipping coffees and nibbling the sweet tarts from the bakery, Ryan cleared his throat, forcing her attention, not that she minded.

"Your sister had a lot of good things to say about you last night," he said.

"Oh, you know that goes." Heidi felt her cheeks warm. "She's my sister. She has to say nice things about me."

"Not really," he said, and Heidi could only shrug because it was true. Not long ago, Bella probably only had bad things to say about her, not that she would have, but she certainly wouldn't have voiced any praise or had reason to either. When she'd first tried working at the bookshop, things had been tense. They'd butted heads. Bella hadn't

wanted to hear Heidi's ideas for the shop any more than Heidi wanted to adhere to Bella's stringent rules without any room for negotiation. Their work relationship had ended quickly, and their personal relationship had taken time to bounce back.

That made her second chance, and Bella's approval, all the more meaningful.

Still, Bella was her sister. Not everyone would be so willing to give Heidi another chance. Not with her resume and work history.

"Doesn't your brother always have nice things to say about you?" Heidi gave him a knowing look, but she was surprised to see him frown a little.

"Not always. Now, sure, but we didn't always have a good relationship, and we're still working on it."

"From what I've seen, you two are tight." Last night they'd laughed together, and at Britt's wedding and its many festivities leading up to it she hadn't picked up on any tension.

"Now, maybe, but I still have a lot to make up for. Truth be told, I'm just happy I have a second chance to make things right."

Heidi knew that the brothers hadn't always been close, but she'd chalked that up to the usual sibling stuff: age and personality differences. Now she wondered if Kyle blamed Ryan for leaving him with the pub all those years, even if he'd never really complained about it, and even if it had almost cost him his marriage at the time.

"It made me wonder..." Ryan seemed to gulp the last of his coffee before he set the mug down heavily on the table. "Would you maybe be willing to give me some thoughts on Harrison's? I'd pay you, of course. But with this ongoing renovation, another opinion might be helpful."

In other words, her opinion might be helpful. But would it? Heidi's heart began to race when she considered the possibility of helping him out with the pub, or somehow making it worse.

But the look he was giving her was so desperate, so nervous, really, that she didn't see how she could let her own insecurity hold her back on this one.

"I can stop by today if that works."

Relief seemed to lighten his expression, pulling his mouth into a grin that, in turn, pulled one from her.

"I'll be there all day," he said. "And...no pressure. It's a tall ask, I know."

Yes and no, Heidi thought. Harrison's Pub needed all the help it could get, and when it came to her resume, so did she.

*

Ryan kept one eye on the door for half the morning, until the lunch crowd shuffled in. Lenny and Walter took their usual seats near the biggest television screen, and Mitch slid them over their beers without needing to take their orders.

Harrison's served dinner only, if you could really call the bar food that, but on Sundays, their father had always kept the kitchen open starting at noon, and as Kyle had done for years, Ryan honored the tradition.

"We have some new menu items you might be interested in, gentlemen," Ryan said, stopping at the bar to hand them the printout of today's specials. Once the menu was finalized, he'd make something nicer, laminated, and more permanent. But this was as good a way as any to see what worked and what didn't. So far, it was mostly a lesson in what didn't.

He could have sworn he saw a smirk pass between the two men when they scanned the menu. Soldiering up with what remained of his pride, Ryan waited pleasantly for a rude comment, and then bid them a good day and carried on. The snickering started by the time he walked to the pool table.

Ignoring it, he did his best to envision how this space would look with more tables. His plan was to push the pool table to the very back of the room, where the old storage rooms had once been before he'd moved everything upstairs. Taking out that additional space and tearing down walls would add a surprising amount of space to the floor plan, and the contractor had shown him the blueprints a few months ago, describing how there could be space for a lounge, and a curtain that could separate the games space from the rest of the bar. Sometimes on a busy night, it was difficult to make conversation over the sound of the balls ricocheting off the table, but then, usually by a certain time of night, the crowd was rowdy and loud. Women tended to cringe when they entered rather than bother to look for a potential mate, which was, far as he could see, the only advantage to attracting so many men to the place.

A low whistle cut through his thoughts and he turned

his attention to follow the sound. Old Lenny was grinning like a Cheshire cat as Heidi walked through the empty dining room, giving both men a menacing stare.

"Cut it out," Mitch said, beating Ryan to it.

"Not too often you see a pretty lady in this place, is all," Walter said, a little shyly.

Now Heidi's expression softened and she gave Ryan a dramatic eye roll.

"They have a point," Ryan admitted, feeling embarrassed by his patrons' behavior.

"Stunts like that don't help," Heidi pointed out. She cast a wide glance around the room and then said, "But I'm a big girl. I can handle a wolf whistle or two. Let them dream."

Ryan fought back a smile. Heidi could hold her own, and she wasn't shy with her opinions, either. He was banking on that.

"I was just showing these gentlemen our specials for the day. Can I interest you in a late lunch?"

Heidi took the menu and studied it. The space between her brow pinched as she read for what felt like a very long time. The silence seemed to fill the bar, as if everyone was waiting for the verdict.

"I grabbed something at the bakery," she said, handing it back to him. "But you know what would go great with this? A Bloody Mary bar, just on Sundays. Do you do other daily specials?"

"Haven't gotten that far." Ryan made a mental note to do that. Immediately.

Heidi pulled in a breath as she looked around. "So, you

did some work on this since Kyle took over. Maybe you could walk me through it?"

He could do that. Ryan started with the most obvious: the windows. While once the dark shutters had blocked out most of the light, giving the space a cavernous feel, whatever the season or time of day, Ryan had them removed to let in the light and, he had hoped, give people on the outside a glimpse in. A reason to enter.

Or not.

He hesitated at the bar, thinking of how he'd planned to sand it down and have it refinished. Recalling what Kyle had told him about the names they'd carved into it, he said, "This is the only thing in here that needs to stay. The bar was important to my father. It has his mark on the place." His, too.

Heidi nodded as he gave her the quick tour, pointing out the additions to the drinks menu, the plans he had for the new space at the back, and of course, the new, more comfortable chairs he'd put at the square tables.

Across the way, the men continued to eye Ryan with suspicious glares.

"I still owe you that ice cream," Ryan said, thinking of a good excuse to leave. And prolong this discussion.

Heidi gave a little smile that he couldn't quite read and said, "I never turn down ice cream, especially on a hot summer day."

The parlor was just down the street and they walked in silence, dodging tourists walking hand in hand, pausing at every storefront to peek in the windows, deciding if they wanted to stop in. Ryan didn't need to get his hopes up that anyone would pop into Harrison's. Not yet anyway.

His spirits lifted when they reached the ice cream shop, and he was pleased to see the line was short for this time of day.

"What'll it be?" he asked Heidi, who still gave him a funny look.

"Mint-chocolate chip," she said. "Two scoops. In a bowl."

"Here I took you for a waffle cone type," he said.

"Don't like the drip. As I said, I do like some neat and order." She grinned and went back outside to find them a table on the sidewalk.

Ryan found her sitting triumphantly at one of the best spots in the shade a few minutes later and handed her the dish and spoon.

"So, what did you think of the pub? And don't worry. I'm a big boy. I can take it." Truthfully, he couldn't, but he didn't really have much choice. He only hoped she saw some hope in it, because he did. He wouldn't have stuck with it otherwise.

"And if you can't take it, you have ice cream to make it all go down a little easier," Heidi said, glancing at him over the table in a way that made this feel like something closer to a conversation between two friends than a business meeting.

"The place has a lot of history," Heidi said, after taking a bite of the ice cream.

"It does," Ryan said, nodding slowly. "My dad loved that bar. It was like his third child. I never really felt that way honestly, and Kyle didn't either. When he took it over, I let him. It wasn't until I moved back here that I realized how much I'd lost by moving away. I wish I'd done things differently, for Kyle, and for my father. This has been my chance to get it right. To make them proud, I guess you could say."

Her eyes softened for a moment as she stared at him, and Ryan pushed back in his chair, thinking he'd gone too far.

"Sounds strange, I know. My dad's been gone a long time by now."

"I don't think it sounds strange at all. You want to honor your father. I get it. I don't think any of us stop wanting to make our parents proud, no matter how old we get. It's not always easy, though."

She frowned as she dragged her spoon through the mint ice cream, and then recovered quickly, "So, what are your thoughts on the place? Kyle kept it exactly the way it always was, and I know that you've had some thoughts about changing it."

"It's a tough balance," Ryan said honestly. "Not everyone embraces the change. But without it…" He grimaced.

"Without it, this place might die along with the guys who kept their tabs open all these years?" Heidi gave a sad smile. "Look, it's your place now. You're still a Harrison, just the next generation. It's okay to move things forward. You can do that and still honor the past."

"I wish I knew how," Ryan said, feeling defeated.

"Take those two guys back there. The cat callers?" Heidi raised an eyebrow and pursed her lips. Despite himself, Ryan let out a laugh. "I'm guessing they're the ones that don't want things to change? They want everything exactly as it was when your dad was pouring the drinks?"

"They're two of them," Ryan said.

"So why not make them feel special? They've been loyal. They're a part of its history. They've heard all the stories. They've kept the place going."

Ryan hadn't thought of it like that, and he was ashamed to realize that. It tapped into some early arguments he'd had when he'd first come back to town and questioned Kyle's management style as much as Kyle defended it.

"Changing things up, catering to tourists or a younger crowd, well, it might make them feel like they're getting pushed out. Like they're not welcome."

"Oh geez." Ryan set his elbows on the table and cupped his head in his hands. "I feel like such a jerk."

"You're not a jerk," Heidi said, looking a little surprised at herself. "I mean...you can come across as one." Her mouth curved slowly into a smile that reached her eyes.

"Gee, thanks." But she had a point. Being reserved had always made him come across as unfriendly. He knew it. He just didn't know how to stop it, exactly. "So what do you propose? About the old-timers?"

Heidi narrowed her eyes in thought. "You mentioned that you were adding more seating. You've changed the chairs already. What about the barstools?"

"Those are on order. I was waiting to decide if I'd refinish the bar first." Before she could ask, he added, "Everything else might change, but that wood, that bar, it has my father's mark on it. It won't be touched."

"Good." She looked so pleased that Ryan felt like he could breathe for the first time in weeks, if not longer. Maybe, just maybe he'd gotten one thing right.

"Those two guys," Heidi said, no doubt referring to Lenny and Walter. "Do they always sit there?"

Ryan nodded. "Always."

"And there they shall always sit," Heidi said. "You leave those stools alone. A couple of others if the need calls for it. And on the back of the wood, you put a small plaque with their names on it. They'll always have a seat at the bar, no matter what else changes."

Ryan stared at her for a beat, long enough for her to look nervous and for her cheeks to go pink.

"Sorry, it was just an idea," she muttered, shaking her head.

"An absolutely brilliant idea," Ryan said, widening his eyes. He marveled for a moment, thinking of how she'd tapped into something he could see but couldn't explain. How she'd found a way to honor the past and keep it alive, without sacrificing progress. And they'd only just gotten started.

"Really?" Heidi looked hesitant across the table.

"Really. I think you could help me turn this place around if you're interested. It would just be for a few weeks until I get a plan in place. Maybe fifteen, twenty hours a week. Name your terms."

"My terms?" She cupped her chin in her hand and thought about it for a minute and then said, "Okay. You host my thirtieth birthday party there. A week from Saturday. That should give us some time to get things moving. Maybe change up the menu, and get the new barstools in. I'll need a signature cocktail if your bartender can do that. And we can talk about the lighting."

"Oh, but I just changed the fixtures," Ryan said.

She gave him a long look. "You'll have to change them again."

Ryan couldn't help but laugh. "You really want your birthday party at Harrison's? But why?"

"Because that place needs a second chance, and people need to give it one." Then, as she stood and extended her hand to shake on the deal, she said, "And because I needed a second chance, too. And you're the only person other than my sister who has been willing to give me one yet."

Ryan slipped his hand around hers, appreciating the warmth of her small palm, and the way her delicate fingers wrapped around his. Something inside his gut twisted at the contact, at the rush of heat that spread up his arm and through his core at the touch.

Because Harrison's wasn't the only place that needed a second chance. She'd given him one, too. She just didn't know it yet.

She lifted her bag higher onto her shoulder and raised her half-eaten cup of ice cream. "And thanks for the ice cream. Especially since you won the bet, not me."

Realizing she was right, Ryan laughed. "Guess you still owe me one, then."

She gave a little smile as she slid her sunglasses onto her face and began walking down the sidewalk. But the truth was, based on everything he'd heard from her just now, he'd be the one owing her before long.

9

Bella had just come back from taking George for a walk when the last of the customers filed out for the day. Heidi was pleased to see that not one, but two people had purchased a copy of the new gardening book that she'd pushed for displaying in the window. With its large scale and glossy photos, the price matched the size, and Heidi made a note on their inventory sheet to order more copies before summer's end.

She paused on that, thinking of what the end of summer would look like. Normally, she looked forward to the change of season, when the tourists went back to their cities and the leaves turned golden and crimson. Now, she knew that it meant more housing would become available. That she or Ryan (preferably him, and likely him) would be moving on and out of the little cottage in the center of town. By then her work at the pub would be finished, too. Essentially, they'd have nothing left to tie them together. They could just go back to cohabiting in the same town, running into each other at family events that crossed over here and there. Normally they didn't even speak, much less interact. He was just a familiar face in the crowd. An extension of her social base, not a part of it.

"Everything okay?"

Heidi hadn't even realized that the trouble she felt was showing on her face. She forced a bright smile at her sister. "Better than okay, actually. You'll be pleased to know that I've found a business in town that wants my help on rebranding."

Bella's eyes popped as she gave George a biscuit. "You're kidding me! I mean, I'm not surprised, but...I guess I didn't think you were very open to it."

It wasn't about not being open to it. It was about whether people would be open to her.

Not wanting to get into that conversation just now, Heidi said, "Well, I couldn't say no on this one. And I didn't want to either."

Bella set George's lead on the hook near the door and then stepped around the counter. "So, are you going to tell me the name of this business?"

"Harrison's," Heidi said casually, but she braced herself for her sister's reaction.

Bella, however, just arched an eyebrow. If Heidi didn't know better, she might say that her sister was impressed.

"That's a pretty big business in town. What does Ryan want you to do?"

What didn't he need her to do, was more like it. Heidi thought about everything they'd discussed on Sunday and just how much work it would entail.

"He's still trying to reinvent the place without losing too much of its history. It's not lost on him that he hasn't exactly widened his customer base as much as he'd hoped. He didn't say as much, but I'm guessing that the day drinkers won't be keeping the lights on much longer."

"Not with the renovations he's been making. That costs money. Even though I'm sure Cole is sticking to the budget as closely as possible, and calling in all the favors, too." Bella pulled in a sigh. "Well, so long as you're sure."

"I'm sure. I just wish I were surer that I could help him turn the place around."

"It can't get much worse than it already is," Bella said.

"I would have thought you'd be more pleased. Isn't this what you've been pushing me to do?" Now it was Heidi's turn to put her sister in the hot seat.

Bella gave a guilty laugh. "True. But I've been encouraging you, not pushing."

Heidi shook her head. "Spoken like a true wordsmith."

"I'm just making sure that it's something you want to do…"

Now Heidi got it, and her face heated with anger that she hadn't caught on earlier. "So I won't walk out on the job a day or two into it? Lose interest, call it quits? Or not give my best effort?"

Darn it. Tears threatened and she hurried away to the back of the shop to tend to the children's corner. It was just as well. There was a story hour later this afternoon. One that her sister now charged a small fee for, which added up and helped the bottom line, all thanks to Heidi's suggestion. She would be taking credit for that.

But there was no use denying that Bella's hesitation came from a true place too.

"Hey, I'm sorry. That's not what I meant, not really." Bella's tone was soft when she came up behind her. "I just want you to follow your passion like you did here in my shop."

Heidi picked up a stuffed animal and set it back on the shelf. They'd decided that moving most of the toys out of reach was best during story-time days. "I think I can help the pub. I want to do it. And it won't interfere with my hours here. It will add to them, perfectly, actually."

They exchanged a little sisterly smile—a truce—and walked back to the counter, where Bella preferred at least one person to be at all times, or at least within reach.

Bella gave a little smile as she began organizing the day's receipts. "You and Ryan seemed to be getting along well at the dinner party the other night."

Heidi swallowed hard and picked up a stack of books to shelve. "Why shouldn't we? As you said, he's harmless."

Bella nodded. "I just didn't think that you agreed with me."

"What can I say? People can change." She was living proof of that. Why should Ryan be the exception?

Because something told her that he wasn't. That he wasn't proud of the man he'd been before coming back to Blue Harbor. That maybe, there was more to his behavior the times she'd observed him, too. That like her, he was fighting to be seen in his family, recognized for an accomplishment, any accomplishment, even if his efforts so far hadn't exactly panned out.

Maybe this was an opportunity for both of them.

Heidi picked up one of the art books and thumbed through it, her pulse quickening on a thought.

She pulled her phone from her pocket and checked the time, then glanced over her shoulder to the counter.

"Mind if I take my break now?"

"It's as good a time as any seeing that we don't have any customers at the moment." Bella gave her a knowing look. "Unless you're trying to get out of story hour."

It was true that story hour wasn't exactly Heidi's favorite part of the week. Passing out juice boxes and paper cups of pretzels and cheese crackers made for a lot of cleanups, too. She might be ready for an actual career and a home of her home...maybe even a relationship, she thought, then pushed that thought away quickly.

But kids? She wasn't going there yet. When she needed a dose, she had her niece Zoe to spoil and pamper.

"Did you give any more thought to my idea about discounting the weekly storybook?" Heidi had watched in frustration for too many weeks as parents shuffled into the store, set their preschoolers up in the children's corner while they relaxed at the back of the room with coffee and talked in hushed voices, and then walked back out again as soon as the final page had been read.

It hadn't been easy to convince Bella that this was a bookstore, not a library. If it hadn't been for her sister's sudden rent increase, maybe Bella wouldn't have been open to hearing her ideas or changing things up around here. Slowly, trust was being earned, and the business had never been better, or so Bella kept saying.

Still, Heidi couldn't take all the credit. This was Bella's shop. She was the one who had to take the risks if Heidi's ideas didn't pan out.

And that was a level of responsibility that made Heidi uneasy, especially when it came to something outside of the family. Her sister would forgive her if she messed up—

something she'd proven by hiring her back after the disastrous first round. Other businesses weren't so accepting, and unfortunately, she'd worked her way through most of Blue Harbor and the surrounding towns, too.

"As a matter of fact, I have the coupons right here." She held up a stack of coupons that Heidi had designed on the computer after last week's story time when not a single person purchased anything after Bella—and George—had entertained their children for nearly an hour. The coupons were visually appealing, meant to cater to the children, if she was being honest—a golden ticket with a cover of this week's book, promised at a ten-percent discount if purchased the same day.

Heidi licked her lip to hide her smile. "Well," she said as she gathered her bag from under the counter. "I hope that we get a few sales out of it."

"Doesn't hurt to try!" Bella tapped them into a neater stack.

"No," Heidi thought, only she still wasn't so sure of that. She was taking a risk, working with Ryan, because if she failed, or didn't live up to his expectations, then she'd just have proven to him that she was the girl everyone thought her to be. And that would hurt. In more ways than one.

*

Kyle stopped by for lunch, as he was known to do from time to time. Ryan had been upstairs most of the morning while Cole and his team got an early start on the former office space. They were putting in the new flooring—not a quiet task—and after closing today the hardwoods in the dining room would be sanded down, removing the scuffed tread and the dark stain.

"Don't mind the dust," he told his brother as they moved to a quieter corner.

"They're making fast progress," Kyle observed. He glanced at Ryan. "Feels a little weird to think that Dad's old office is gone. I spent a lot of time in that room over the years."

Ryan felt uneasy as he unwrapped the sandwiches that Kyle had carried over from the deli. He knew that his brother was fine with him taking over the place, but years of tension still lingered, not completely forgotten, even if they'd been resolved this past year.

"The door's always open to you here if you want to team up," he said now, even though he knew that Kyle wouldn't take him up on that offer—and that there wasn't enough payroll to go around for the both of them either at the moment.

"Thanks, but I'm pretty happy at the moment. Not that I was completely unhappy here." He gave a little smile that didn't quite meet his eyes. "It was bittersweet, you could say."

Ryan nodded. He understood. Still, he needed to be sure.

"Do you ever regret leaving this place?" Ryan ventured. It had been over a year since he'd come back to town, roughly a full year since Ryan had taken full ownership of the family business. He knew that Kyle had felt burdened by it for years, that it had cost him his own plans and nearly his marriage, and that Ryan probably should have stepped in and shared his brunt of the responsibility sooner. Now, though, he saw something sentimental pass through Kyle's gaze.

"You know what they say about absence making the heart go fonder." Kyle bit into his sandwich and chewed thoughtfully. "Running this place had its upside, but I'm happier doing what I love, being with the woman I love, and knowing that Dad's legacy has been put in trusted hands."

"About that." Ryan wondered if now was as good a time as any to broach the topic. "I'm going to be making a lot of changes around here. I know you said I had your blessing." He also knew that his ideas for change had initially been met with heavy resistance from Kyle. "But I want to keep this place in the family. I want to still make it true to our roots."

"Okay." Kyle stared at him for a moment. "Something I should know? You aren't going to paint the walls pink or anything?"

Ryan laughed, thinking that even had been surprisingly respectful of his vision for the place, keeping change thoughtful and minimal, but enough that it could give people a reason to stop inside, and see what was new.

"I'm replacing all the tables. The new chairs don't look right with them." He motioned to the new ones. Steel. Farmhouse meets industrial style, or so Heidi had said in a detailed plan that she'd left for him to find this morning, next to the coffeepot. She was right. The glossy black tables full of scuffs and scrapes stood out like a sore thumb.

"I was wondering if you might make the new tables," he said. "Name your price. If you have the time, of course." He saw the hesitancy in his brother's eyes and knew that he was asking for a lot.

"Are you kidding me? I'll make the time!" Kyle grinned. "On one condition."

"Name it."

"You let me give you the family discount," Kyle said.

Ryan shook his head and took a big bite of his sandwich, feeling hungrier than he had in a while. Motivation did that. "I'm paying full price."

"I'm not taking your money," Kyle replied, leaning back in his chair.

They were at an impasse. Only unlike when they were growing up, this was an argument that stemmed from kindness and respect, not resentment and jealousy.

"Then let me put it in an account for my future niece or nephew." Ryan watched Kyle waver. Pushing the topic, he warned, "College is mighty expensive these days."

"Fine," Kyle grumbled. "But only if you take the family discount."

Ryan saw this as a compromise. "It's a deal."

"What's a deal?" a voice asked from behind him. Ryan turned to see Heidi standing in the doorway of the pub, a large leather tote bag hung on her slim shoulder. She was dressed more professionally than he was used to seeing her, in a navy-blue sundress and pink cardigan. His gaze floated down to her long, bare legs where they stopped at her simple flats. Ballet flats, they were called. And his ex-girlfriend liked to wear them too.

Pulling himself together, he gave a pleasant grin and said, "To what do I owe the honor? Unless?" Unless? "You're here to enjoy the ambiance and a drink?"

"It's barely past noon," Heidi said with a laugh. She glanced at old Lenny and Walter at the bar top. "Not that I'm passing judgment, but I am on my lunch break and I don't think Bella would be all too pleased with me if I came back tipsy."

"Heidi's going to be working with me on some ideas for the place," Ryan told Kyle, whose eyes widened in surprise. "It was actually Heidi's idea to ask you to do the tables."

"So you got my note?" Heidi beamed, and the look wasn't lost on Kyle.

His grin was obvious enough for Ryan to shoot him a warning glance. As Heidi approached the table, Ryan pulled over an extra chair. "I was just telling Kyle about our thoughts for the tables."

Heidi's eyes lit up as she inched her chair closer to the table and hooked her bag over the back of it. "Wonderful! I think that something rustic will bring some character to this place. Give it that touch of warmth that people seem to crave. I'll put together some more lighting options later on now that we know we're going to have such beautiful, wooden tables."

"Preference on the stain?" Kyle looked only slightly amused as Heidi tipped her head and thought about it.

"I trust your judgment. You're the craftsman, and you know this place as well as anyone. Better, I suppose. We're trying to lighten it up, but we don't want it to feel too modern. This is an old place, full of character, and it's important to keep that charm."

Ryan felt uneasy as he took a bite of his sandwich. It was true that Kyle did know this place best, and Ryan was still learning the ropes. He knew that Kyle would freely give advice if he asked for it, but he also knew that Kyle kept a lot of his opinions to himself, as part of this new relationship they had formed. Gone were the days of competing for their father's affection. Now it was just the two of them, and their mother.

Scratch that. Kyle had Brooke. And a baby on the way.

"I don't have much time," Heidi confessed, standing up. "I was stopping by to see if you wanted to grab a coffee with me before I get back to the bookstore."

Ryan felt his brother's eyes drilling into him from across the table. He kept his eyes on his sandwich, waiting to see if there would be a kick under the table.

"I can see you're busy, though, so another day."

"I have to get going soon, actually," Kyle said, starting to wrap up his sandwich.

"Nonsense. I don't have much time anyway. Just thought I'd run a few ideas past you about my party." She turned to Kyle and said, "You and Brooke will be invited of course. My big three-oh. A week from Saturday night."

"Here?" Kyle looked as shocked as most people probably would.

But Heidi just shrugged. "Why not? It's time to change people's perceptions of this place, and I can't think of a better opportunity, can you? And no rush on the tables, well, not really. I assume that Ryan's willing to pay extra for expedited service? At least for a portion of the order?"

By the time she'd walked out the door, Kyle's shoulders were shaking in laughter.

"What's so funny?" Ryan asked, taking a big bite of his sandwich and resisting the urge to glance out the window and watch Heidi disappear from sight.

"First you're living together—"

"We're not living together," Ryan corrected.

Kyle's expression said otherwise. "Now you're working together."

"I just—" He stopped himself there. Kyle's mischievous smirk was growing into a full-blown grin. There was no point in arguing with him when he got like this, much like he'd done as a kid when they argued about something stupid and he was the one who always got worked up while Kyle let it roll off him.

Besides, what he said was sort of true. Even if it was all just temporary.

Ryan watched as Kyle wrapped up his sandwich and pushed back his chair. "Where are you going?"

"More like where are *you* going?" Kyle said. "I'm going to stop by Brooke's shop and see if she'd like the rest of this sandwich, now that she's eating for two. And you are on your way to the bakery if I'm not mistaken."

Without another word, he gave Ryan a nod and moved toward the door. His laughter could be heard through the window until he was out of sight.

Ryan stared at his sandwich and then checked his watch. A quick coffee might taste good. And the conversation could be helpful.

And who was he kidding?

Certainly not his kid brother.

*

Buttercream Bakery was buzzing, like it was most days, from the time that it opened for the early morning crowd until they sold their very last muffin.

Maddie Conway handed over a white bakery bag to a woman with a baby stroller and greeted Heidi with a smile. "No Bella today?"

Often, Bella stopped in for a quick lunch, even if she brought it back to the shop. But today, Heidi hadn't exactly invited her along.

"She has the kids coming in for story time," Heidi explained.

Maddie's grin turned knowing. "Ah. Perfect timing for you, then."

Heidi felt like a bit of a heel, but Bella had been wrangling those children long before she'd brought Heidi in to help her with the shop. "I think I'll take her back a rosemary scone if you have any left."

"I always set one aside for Bella." Maddie added one to a bag. "Now what can I get for you?"

Heidi looked at the options, which filled the display case, the baskets, and the glass domes that rested on top.

"Would it be wrong to eat a slice of cake for lunch?"

Maddie looked at her frankly. "I own a bakery. Cake at any hour is acceptable to me. Besides, that's one of the perks that come with being an adult, right? You might get stuck with bills and all those other pesky responsibilities, but if you want to live off ice cream, cake, and candy, no one can stop you."

"I like your attitude," Heidi said with a laugh. "I'm sure the local dentist does too."

Maddie winked. "He's my best customer."

Heidi looked at the cake selections, feeling her stomach grumble. "They all look so good that it's hard to choose."

"Then try them all and let me know which one you like best. You do plan to have a birthday cake for your party?"

"Of course," Heidi said, getting excited at the thought even though it was a detail she hadn't considered yet. The venue was a top priority at the moment. "And a coffee too, please." That was the real point of coming in here today: caffeine. Well, that and talking to Ryan about the pub.

So far two things had gone off-plan. It was probably for the best that she was never one of those scheduling types with lists and folders.

"Are you hosting at your house again?" Maddie plated three thin, but not too thin, slices of cake on a hand-painted vintage plate and reached for a mug.

"It's going to be at Harrison's," Heidi replied, eyeing the cake. She managed to keep herself from dipping her finger into the creamy chocolate frosting of the vanilla sponge cake.

"Harrison's?" Maddie didn't hide her disgust. "I thought you'd say the Carriage House. Or Firefly. Or your lovely new backyard again." She tipped her head. "Honey, why don't you just have it here? I'm usually sold out before dinnertime and I can clear away some tables and bring in some food from next door."

While Amelia's food and this beautiful setting were a little more in line with how Heidi had always pictured her thirtieth birthday, she shook her head. "It's going to be at Harrison's, but don't worry, it will be a nice time, I promise.

I'm actually consulting on the new plans for the place." She couldn't keep the pride out of her voice, even though she still felt a little out of place with such an announcement.

"Wow." Maddie looked impressed. "Cole didn't tell me yet."

"It was just decided yesterday," Heidi explained.

"Well, between your input and Cole's handiwork, there might just be hope for the place yet. I'd love to give it another try, but until they make the atmosphere and the drink list more desirable, I feel bad saying that it's just not my scene."

It wasn't Heidi's either, but that didn't mean the place was hopeless.

"I'll let you know more about the party details later in the week," Heidi promised as a patron behind cleared her throat with impatience. Exchanging a secret smile with Maddie, Heidi scooted to the side and nearly collided with Ryan, who had just stepped through the door.

"Whoa," he said, taking a step back. His expression turned to one of amusement when his gaze fell on the plate in her hands. "That's a lot of cake."

"I'm taste-testing for my party," she told him, even though the slices were hardly sample sizes. "There's plenty to share if you want to grab an extra fork?"

She realized her error immediately. The man was too uptight to eat ice cream out of a carton without some serious cajoling. No doubt he'd be horrified at the thought of sharing food off a single plate.

But to her surprise, he said, "That's an offer I can't resist." He leaned over to the coffee station and grabbed a plastic fork. "So was meeting you here."

Heidi's cheeks burned. "Oh?"

"Yeah, I can't wait to hear your ideas for the pub."

Oh. Unsure why she felt a strange sense of disappointment at his reasons for meeting, she lifted her chin toward the door. "Let's sit outside, I've been cooped up all day."

The deck of Buttercream Bakery extended all the way down to its neighboring business, the Firefly Café, and had a sweeping view of Lake Huron. Both Maddie and her sister Amelia extended the life of the patio for as far into the cold season as they could, first with heat lamps, and then with igloos, where diners could enjoy the picturesque surroundings without enduring the Northern Michigan elements. Winter was harsh this far north, there was no denying that, but the lake never failed to impress. Sometimes, Heidi even thought it was prettiest when the town was covered in snow.

A woman and two children were just getting up—probably to hurry over to story time at Bella's Books—and Ryan took quick strides to grab the table. He held out a chair for her and then took a seat for himself.

Chivalrous. She'd give him that.

"So, what was this big idea you had?"

Heidi picked up her fork. "Oh, no. Cake first. Then business."

Waiting for protest, she was surprised that Ryan pulled the plate closer and took a big chunk of the lemon chiffon with a blueberry filling.

"Oh, that's good. I don't think I've tried this before, but then, I don't really eat much outside of the pub and take-out."

"And my delicious chicken," Heidi joked. She went for the chocolate cake first. Maddie had added a hint of raspberry and chocolate chunks. It was rich but not too sweet. Something about Ryan's comment nagged at her while she sipped her coffee, amused to see that Ryan dared to try a taste of the chocolate, where her fork had already been.

"What about the Carriage House Inn?" she asked. "You don't eat there?" It was hands down the most popular spot in town. The pub just off the lobby of the quaint establishment was crowded year-round, indoors and out, drawing locals and tourists alike.

"Oh, well, everyone goes to the Carriage House Inn." Ryan's jaw seemed to tense as set his fork down.

"You can't compete with that place," Heidi agreed. She looked at him squarely. "And you shouldn't try to. They have their own specialties, their own attractions. We need to find something that makes Harrison's unique."

"I'm all ears." Ryan looked at her so openly, that she realized just how much her opinion counted.

She swallowed hard, not wanting to mess this up or get ahead of herself, as she was known to do with some of her grand ideas that hadn't exactly panned out in the past. Her parents had a box of perfume-making supplies to prove it.

"What if you feature a different artist's work on your walls, say once a month? There are tons of talented artists in the area, and most of what they paint is based on this beautiful scenery." She swept her hand over the view to underscore her point. "Take Ellie Morgan, for example. She used to run an art class over on Evening Island and her watercolors are stunning. So bright and full of color. And

I'm sure Mila would be thrilled to have some of her work exposed like that too—and her students." The art studio here in town offered classes to children, and Heidi knew that her niece Zoe very much enjoyed them, even if Heidi did have a rather difficult time understanding what she was looking at half the time and relied on Natalie to inform her that the green blob was a "brilliant frog" or the like.

"It would certainly add color to the walls," Ryan said slowly. It was clear that he was thinking about it, but not completely sold.

"And it would drive new business," Heidi pointed out. "The artists would bring their friends and families, and if they like the place enough, they'll come back. You could even host a special event, say once a month, when you debuted that artist's work. That would really pull in a crowd. We could make it invite-only. People don't like to feel left out and it will make them want to come to Harrison's more than ever, even if they have to wait for the next event."

Ryan seemed to warm up to the idea a little more. "And featuring local art will keep the place authentic. True to its roots."

"Exactly. Harrison's is the heart of your family. Why not make it the heart of the town, too?"

His mouth slowly curved into a grin so broad that Heidi felt herself blush. "I think I might have underestimated you," he said.

She couldn't completely accept the compliment, not when she was guilty of the same. "And people have underestimated your business, too. We'll get it back on track. And I have one more idea for that." She hesitated. "You said you don't get much, but it's time to change that. This weekend, you and I are going to all the dining options in town, and the bars, too. We're going to see firsthand what works and what doesn't. And what you could be doing differently."

"It's not a bad idea." Ryan looked at her carefully. "And most of the construction will be done by then so the timing works. So, we'll have dinner together? Drinks?"

"If you think it's a good idea," she replied. Her heart was beginning to pound.

He picked up his fork and took another bite of cake. The lemon this time. "I think…it's a date."

10

Heidi was relieved that Ryan was working at Harrison's all day and that they'd be meeting at their first stop—the Firefly Café. Anything more, like leaving the house together, would have felt too personal. Like a date.

Like Ryan had said.

Figure of speech, she told herself as she switched out her everyday earrings for something a little more sparkly. It was Saturday night in the summer in Blue Harbor and she was about to hit some of the best spots in town. That was reason enough to wear her favorite black sundress and strappy gold sandals. There was absolutely nothing more to it. After all, she and Ryan had managed to spend hours together each afternoon that week, brainstorming ideas for the pub, chatting with Cole about the finishing touches on the renovation, and tasting new samples from the cook. They were coworkers, in a sense. Roommates.

Maybe, even friends.

But nothing more. Certainly. Ryan Harrison? She nearly laughed out loud at the thought.

Grabbing her denim jacket and a hair tie that she slipped onto her wrist, Heidi hurried down the hall and locked the front door behind her. The walk to the Firefly Café was short, and outside the crickets had started to hum

as evening fell. Still, the air was warm, even as the lake breeze picked up when she made her way down the path toward the café, and there was a warm glow in the sky that promised a beautiful sunset.

Ryan was already waiting for her on the front step when she arrived at the end of the gravel path.

"I wasn't sure if we should eat outside or in," he said, his gaze lazily sweeping over her.

She told herself it was just the outfit. The man was used to seeing her in sweats, after all.

Still, her stomach fluttered a little. "And here I thought you were just dodging Candy," she teased. "But I think we should eat inside. Get the full experience."

"If you're up for it," Ryan warned with a lift of his eyebrows. "Candy's already seen me through the window and I've seen her crane her neck more than once to see who I'm waiting for."

"Oh, she's harmless," Heidi said, taking the next step. And nothing she couldn't handle.

Still, she braced herself for what the woman would say when she saw the two of them together. No doubt she'd assume there was more to the situation than there was, because Candy saw love and romance blooming at every turn, and she certainly wouldn't rest until every Conway and Clark girl was happily matched up and married.

Heidi could only hope that Amelia's upcoming wedding and Bella's baby announcement would keep her occupied for a while, or at least for tonight.

Alas, that hope blew away in the breeze as soon as Ryan opened the door and they both stepped inside the warm and inviting room that was already filled with customers leaning over their tables, engaged in happy conversation, many sharing a bottle of wine and an appetizer.

"Why Heidi and Ryan Harrison! Now isn't that a unique pairing!" Candy's voice boomed loud enough to draw the attention of several patrons.

"I changed my mind. Maybe we should eat outside," Heidi hissed to Ryan.

Maybe, they should have skipped this place altogether. While popular, it was a friendly family diner, not a pub or a bar, whereas Harrison's would always cater to a later night crowd, adults only.

Still, it was popular, the food was excellent, and Amelia had found a way to preserve the history of the place when she took it over several years back.

"Hello, Candy," Heidi said with a practiced smile as the woman came to pull her into a long, squishy hug. Heidi had to admit that it did feel good. While unavoidable, Candy was at least a very good hugger.

Releasing her, Candy trained her eyes on Ryan. "Don't you clean up well!"

Ryan looked down at his outfit—khaki pants and a button-down shirt—and frowned as he ran a hand down his flat stomach. "I always dress like this, Candy."

That part was true, mostly, but Heidi had also seen a more casual side to him. Maybe, a different side altogether.

"Oh, I made you blush," Candy apologized to Ryan, whose cheeks turned redder. "I know what will take away these first date jitters. A bottle of Conway wine. On the house!"

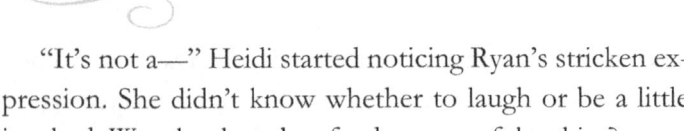

"It's not a—" Heidi started noticing Ryan's stricken expression. She didn't know whether to laugh or be a little insulted. Was the thought of a date so awful to him?

And moreover, why wasn't the thought of a date so awful to her?

"Pick any open table you'd like and I'll be right back," Candy promised with a waggle of her eyebrows.

"I'm sorry." Heidi winced at Ryan as soon as they were seated at a table near the windows with a view of the dining room as well as the patio. It also gave a vantage point of the kitchen through the pass, and right now Heidi could see Amelia and Candy arm-wrestling over a bottle of wine that she assumed was intended for their table.

"It's all part of the charm of this place," Ryan said with a grin. "If this café can pull in this much business with Candy at the helm, then I don't see why Harrison's can't make it, too."

Heidi watched as Amelia came to their table with a bottle of wine and two glasses, her cheeks flushed and her eyes bright. Her strawberry blonde hair showed signs of exertion. Or a struggle.

"Hello, friends," she said with a warm smile. "I hear I missed a great dinner party last weekend."

Now it was Heidi's turn to blush. "Oh, it was just a casual get-together."

"It was a wonderful time," Ryan corrected, giving her a pointed look across the table.

Heidi felt the heat in her cheeks crank up a notch. "Next time we'll do it on a Sunday, so you can join us," she promised Amelia, only realizing that there may not be a next time, or maybe, no reason for there not to be one.

Amelia looked pleased with the prospect of the invitation. "To what do I owe the honor of having you two here tonight?"

Heidi struggled to think of an explanation, but Ryan quickly said, "Thought I'd check out your secret sauce. You've got quite an operation here."

"It's certainly busy, especially on weekends in the summer," Amelia said as she popped the cork on the bottle with an expert hand. Having grown up at Conway Orchard and Winery, she'd helped her father through every step of the process from harvesting to labeling. It was her late mother who had inspired both her and Amelia to pursue the culinary arts, though.

She poured them each a glass. "If you were to ask Candy, she would say that she's the secret behind the sauce."

Heidi gave Amelia a knowing smile. "She certainly keeps things interesting. Tell me, is she still trying to design your wedding dress?"

"And the bridesmaid dresses and take over the flowers." Amelia shook her head. "I'm so busy that I appreciate the help and I have to admit that she is very good at what she does." She lowered her voice. "And it does keep her out of the kitchen for a bit."

Ryan and Heidi were still chuckling when Amelia left to take the orders from guests who had just arrived.

"Should we toast?" Heidi asked, raising her glass.

Ryan tipped his head. "To…the summer. A summer of…second chances."

She smiled all the way down to her chest as she clinked

his glass. "I like that," she said, taking a long sip of the smooth red wine.

She felt his stare over the rim of her wineglass before he took a sip from his own glass.

"I like that we're doing this," he said.

Heidi picked up the menu and studied it intently, even though she had it completely memorized a long time ago, right down to Amelia's weekly specials.

She liked that they were doing this too. And she wasn't so sure that she should.

*

By the time they'd finished dinner at the café and moved on to a few other pubs and bars in the area, Ryan had almost forgotten that this was technically a research trip. Heidi was an easy person to talk to, always quick with a story or a laugh, never one to sit in silence for long, something that used to annoy him but now something he found he appreciated. Even enjoyed.

They settled into a table at the Yacht Club for their last call, considered to be the nicest of the options in Blue Harbor and the neighboring town of Pine Falls.

"I'm not keeping you out too late, am I?" Heidi asked as she studied the menu.

He gave her a hard look even as he struggled to fight a grin. "I'm not that old."

"Forty, right?" She struggled against a smile.

"Very funny," he said, setting down the drinks menu, which was a little too complicated for his taste. "Though I suppose that's only fair considering I accused you of barely being drinking age. However," he said, pointing at her. "You should have taken that as a compliment."

Even if at the time, it might not have been intended as one, he thought, feeling bad.

"Age is just a number," Heidi said. "Or at least I tell myself with my birthday around the corner." She sighed as she shrugged into her denim jacket and tossed her hair back over the collar. A few strands remained tucked in and Ryan resisted the urge to reach out and pull them free. To touch her.

"I need to make this decade better than the last. There are a lot of things that I wish I'd done differently."

"Doesn't everyone feel that way?" Ryan paused that thought while a young waiter took their order. Like everyone else on staff, he was dressed in a crisp white polo with striped seersucker shorts, a look that underscored the nautical theme of the place and its prime position on the water, looking out onto Evening Island over the wide-open waters of Lake Huron. During the summer days, there were Adirondack chairs set up over its lush green grass, where guests could sip cocktails while enjoying the view, or play lawn games. In the winter the space was used for bonfires, with paper lanterns creating a magical setting in the snow.

They'd made the place a destination. Ryan couldn't help but feel discouraged when he thought of the run-down place on Main Street that he'd inherited.

"So, what is it that you would change?" Heidi asked, spreading her elbows on the table as she leaned in. There was a hint of mischief in her eyes that he'd come to appreciate. She wasn't just a good-time girl. She was fun. And easy to talk to.

And conversation had never come easily to him.

"I probably wouldn't have moved to Cleveland." It wasn't the first time he'd thought this, but the regret still lingered heavily in his chest. "I wasn't here for my family the way I could have been. When my dad passed away, Kyle was left to take care of everything, and I just…" He clenched his jaw, feeling the same shame that he couldn't shake, no matter how much he'd repaired his relationship with Kyle. "I just kept living my life."

"But it all worked out in the end," Heidi said brightly. "Brooke has moved back to town, and now she has a shop here that's thriving. My cousins and aunt and uncle are thrilled that she's putting down roots here. If you'd been the one to take over the bar back then, then Kyle would have moved to New York. They'd probably still be there."

Ryan hadn't thought about it like this. "You're an eternal optimist, you know that?"

Heidi shrugged. "I just try not to let things bog me down too much. That's not always a good thing, at least according to my family."

"So what is it that you'd change?" he asked, genuinely curious. Sometimes, it was easy to assume that he was the only person with regrets.

Heidi looked up as the waiter approached with their drinks and then took a sip of her cocktail. "Oh, this is good. Here, take a sip."

Ryan hesitated, realizing that sharing food was something that Heidi did on a regular basis, even if he wasn't used to sharing much of anything. Not his home. Not his food. Certainly not his feelings.

Now, he was doing all three.

The drink was smooth, slightly sweet, and warm as it chased its way down his throat. "Not bad."

In other words, it made everything that didn't come straight from a bottle or can at Harrison's taste like medicine.

"Remember that, because you're going to have a list of signature cocktails at Harrison's."

Ryan grinned. "I can't believe I never thought of that before."

Heidi just shrugged again. "You were too close to it to see what was missing."

Ryan nodded thoughtfully, taking in her pretty mouth and the way her eyes lit up in the candlelight. "It's easy to overlook what's right in front of you," he said, and then, when their eyes met, quickly took a sip of his own drink. A beer, and one that he intended to nurse so he was on top of his game tomorrow.

And so he didn't do anything stupid, like go and kiss this beautiful woman sitting across from him.

"Back to what you'd change," he said, clearing his throat.

"Oh, I probably would have given a little more thought to my career path rather than just trying everything until something finally stuck." Heidi chewed her lip. "I don't have the best reputation in town. People sort of view me as a quitter, even though that's not the case. I knew what wasn't working and when to walk away. Sometimes it was sooner than people would have liked."

"That's not a bad quality," Ryan said, raising his

eyebrows. "In fact, I wish that I'd walked away from situations earlier rather than sticking them out, hoping they would become more fulfilling. You listened to your gut. Life is too short to waste time on the wrong things or people."

"I almost believe you," Heidi said, but there was a smile in her eyes that hadn't been there a moment ago. "What didn't work for you in Cleveland?"

Ryan hesitated. "Everything." He laughed, even though it wasn't very funny. "I didn't see it at first, or maybe at first, everything was fine. I had a great job, I was dating a woman I thought I might end up marrying. My life felt steady, the way I like it."

But it also felt boring, he realized, looking back. And more than anything, it felt empty.

There was no family. His position at the accounting firm was replaceable, and he had no emotional ties to the work. And as for his love life...that wasn't really love at all, was it? It was companionship. It was safe. And when it ended it had nearly broken him.

"And then what happened?"

He gave her a wry grin. "Then...I got dumped. Left for my boss, of all people."

"Ouch." Heidi grimaced and took another sip of her drink. He followed suit.

"Yeah. That was my cue to exit. Looking back, there were a lot of reasons to leave earlier, but I just didn't see it until it was right in my face."

"And now you're back in Blue Harbor, and this is your first night out in a year."

Now Ryan really laughed, hard and loud. "I'm not the bore everyone paints me out to be. I took over a failing business. In truth, it's still failing. I'm putting everything I have into that place, with my time and my money. It's...it's my priority right now."

He omitted the part that other than the occasional night with the guys, he preferred his own company. A quiet night after a long day. The safety in knowing that he wouldn't make a wrong move again, fall for the wrong girl, or worse, be rejected.

Just like he didn't admit that he had been lonely, that his life had been emptier than he'd realized. That it wasn't until he started coming home to Heidi, seeing her on a daily basis, that he realized how nice it was to have someone in his life again.

Even if she was just passing through.

*

The night was still warm when they made it back to the cottage. It was late, even for her, but she knew she wouldn't sleep well tonight, even if she tried. Something was shifting between the two of them. Something unexpected, maybe even something good. And she wasn't ready for the night to end just yet. Even though it probably should.

"Big day tomorrow?" she said, once Ryan had unlocked the door and let her pass through.

"Cole's going to come around, even though it's Sunday. He wants to make sure everything is finished before your party next weekend."

"Our party," she reminded him, easing off her shoes. "It will be a big reveal for the pub. You nervous?"

Ryan hesitated and she waited. The Ryan she knew until now would shake his head, say absolutely not, give nothing away.

His gaze slid to her and he grinned. "Probably won't sleep all week."

"In that case…" She walked into the kitchen, returning with two bowls of ice cream and two spoons. Ryan was already settled on a couch, scrolling through his phone. He looked up when she settled onto a chair and handed him a bowl. "I don't think I'll get much sleep tonight either."

"Something on your mind?"

Heidi swallowed back a bite of ice cream. "Oh…lots of things. Life feels really unsettled at the moment, but it also feels like it suddenly has a lot of possibilities."

"I would think you'd find that to be a good thing."

He'd be right about that, proving that maybe he did know her for who she really was. Still…she knew better than to get ahead of herself. She'd had enough setbacks and disappointments not to get too hopeful.

"Sometimes it's scary, though, right?"

Their gazes snagged and then locked for a moment, and Heidi felt her chest begin to pound. Quickly, she looked down at her ice cream, which was beginning to melt in the bowl, just the way she preferred it.

"Oh, I should get to bed. I'm opening the shop tomorrow," she said, even though that wasn't until ten.

"I should too," Ryan said, and then seemed to sit back down again when she stood. He cleared his throat, clearly suddenly feeling as awkward as she did. "So, we'll work out the schedule for this week?"

"It will be a big week," she said, inching toward the kitchen. And it would be, not just because of all she had to do for her party. The lights were coming, the new lounge furniture too, and after seeing the staff at the Yacht Club, she needed to have a word with Ryan about the uniforms at the pub.

But not tonight. No, tonight she needed to get to bed, even if she only stared at the ceiling and listened for sounds of Ryan from across the hall.

"You can use the bathroom first if you'd like," Ryan said when she came out of the kitchen just as he was entering.

She looked up at him, wondering why the night was taking an awkward shift and knowing that it couldn't be the reason she thought it was—if anything, just the opposite. She and Ryan were coworkers, roommates, and nothing more than that. And tonight, and all the other times, were just an extension of this new shift in their relationship.

Ryan was probably worried she was getting the wrong idea. And she was just as worried that he was too. Yes, that was definitely it.

"I think I'll let you go first. I don't want to have to worry about leaving water around the sink," she teased.

"Oh, you only do that some of the time." His mouth curved into a smile.

"And let me guess?" Heidi tipped her head. "You wipe it down with a towel?"

His jaw twitched. "Guilty as charged."

She laughed and walked back into the living room, sensing him behind her. "Why am I not surprised?" Except that she was, for many reasons.

Because he could have called her out on it, given it a reason for a typical roommate tiff—they weren't unheard of and she'd had her share over the years.

Instead, he'd taken care of her. Accepted her for who she was.

"Thanks for sharing some of your ice cream," he said, pausing outside his bedroom door. It was clear that there was more he wanted to say. "You don't need to label all your food, by the way. I promise I won't eat it."

Heidi laughed again, shaking her head. "Sorry about that. I've had roommates before and…force of habit. But as roommates go, I'd have to say that you're one of the best I've ever had."

A look passed over his face as he opened his door. "So you don't regret not taking the mouse-infested place with the pea-green carpet?"

"Oh, I have lots of regrets, but that's not one of them," she told him.

And neither, she thought, once they both entered their own bedrooms and closed the doors, did she regret ending up in this cottage with him.

Her only regret now was that it was only for the summer.

11

By the time Heidi's birthday rolled around, she was nearly as nervous about greeting her guests as Ryan was about letting them into the pub, though, unlike Ryan, she wasn't visibly pacing up and down the length of the newly polished flooring, checking to make sure that every votive candle was indeed lit.

They'd been working together for the past two hours to get everything set up. The new lounge furniture had arrived yesterday and was now set up in the space that had once been the back office. With the pool table shielded by the thick, navy velvet curtain that led to the former back office and storage space, the main floor looked spacious and inviting. Kyle had delivered a dozen tables over the course of the week, and even though there were more to come over the next month, for now, they brightened the space with the lighter wood tones that matched the new light fixtures that had been installed with Cole's expertise.

The upgraded barstools matched the chairs, giving the bar a modern feel, and for tonight only, the old chairs that would be reserved exclusively for the oldest and most loyal of patrons had been tucked away safely in the upstairs office area.

The sun was setting out the large windows and the

lampposts on Main Street were just beginning to glow. There was a warm and inviting mood to the space that hadn't been there before—at least not to Heidi's demographic.

"If Lenny were here tonight, he'd have something to say about these flower arrangements," Ryan said, raking a nervous hand through his hair.

"Well, it's my party and there will be flowers if I want them," Heidi teased. She swept her eyes over the tables and bar area, where matching mixed bouquets added a much-needed splash of color to the otherwise wood-toned room. Ryan had picked them up himself rather than let Gabby deliver them to the pub, claiming he didn't want to spoil the reveal.

Now, Heidi saw that Gabby had included all of her favorite flowers in each bouquet, even though she still couldn't name them all. Sure, it was Gabby's business to observe these things, which was what made all of the birthday and anniversary bouquets she designed so personal and perfect, but it also reminded Heidi of what a special community this was. One where everyone pulled together.

Even her and Ryan Harrison, of all people.

"Well, my dress matches the flowers," she said, bending down to sniff a few.

She caught Ryan staring at her when she straightened and only then realized that while she had been talking to herself, he'd overheard.

"You look really nice," he said now.

She glanced down at her light pink dress and smoothed her ponytail. "You clean up pretty well yourself."

"But I'm wearing what I always wear," he said with a laugh.

"You're forgetting that I've seen your flannels," she reminded him. "I know there's a whole other side to you."

Clearing her throat against the intensity of his stare, she motioned to the room. "It looks lovely. Lively. Inviting. Once there's some artwork on the walls, it will feel more complete, but for now, I think we've pulled it off."

"I'll wait to see how tonight goes before I pop the champagne," Ryan said as he began straightening already straight chairs.

"Oh, you will be popping the champagne much sooner than that. It is my birthday, after all," she reminded him.

"I just hope it's a good one." He'd moved all around the room, coming finally to stand beside her. She rested a hand on his arm. "It will be."

Something passed between them and she realized that she was still holding onto him. Dropping her arm quickly, she walked over to the bar and surveyed the trays of appetizers—simple, bite-size snacks that were just a sample of what would soon be on the new menu. Each one looked more delicious than the next.

"You still think we got the menu right?"

With her back to him, Heidi couldn't help but grin. "You've only asked that thirty-five times." Heidi turned and popped a bacon-wrapped date into her mouth. "In the past half hour."

Their eyes met briefly and his mouth curved into a smile. "I just want everything to be perfect. For the guests…and for you. It's your birthday and you've made

this place into something more than I could have done on my own, and in a very short amount of time."

"We make a pretty good team," Heidi said quietly.

"Someday I'll find a way to thank you," he said.

She finished chewing, her pulse quickening when she considered what he meant by that, if there would be another reason to get together, for drinks at the Yacht Club, for dinner at the Firefly Café, or just out on the back deck at the house they shared.

A knock at the glass-paned door made her jump.

There was no time for thinking about any of that now. Friendly faces smiled through the window, holding up gift bags, and waving in greeting.

Their guests had arrived. And by the end of the night, they'd know for certain if they were a good team…or not.

*

Bella was the first one to approach Heidi, and not just to wish her a happy birthday. "Look at this place!"

Heidi beamed with pride, even though it wasn't her pub or her business. She felt a connection to it. And to the owner.

"Looks a lot better, huh?"

"You did amazing work," Bella said.

"Don't forget Cole," Maddie added. She was holding a giant bakery box and lifted it in the air. "Where do you want this, Heidi?"

"Oh, over on the bar makes sense," Heidi said. "I can't wait to see what you've done, Maddie."

"You'll be more interested in seeing Brooke and Kyle's

cake next weekend," Maddie said excitedly. "They're having a gender reveal party at the Firefly Café, and only I know the secret."

"You mean you're not even going to give us a hint?" Heidi didn't care to guess, though. She liked surprises, and the thought of another party—and another excuse to spend some time with Ryan.

"Good thing Candy isn't here or she'd be dragging it out of you," Bella said with a laugh.

"That's the reason why Brooke hasn't sent out the invitations yet. It's a word-of-mouth thing and she's hoping that Candy will be the last to know."

"Considering the party is being held at the café where Candy works, that's unlikely. But worth a try." The women all laughed and moved toward the bar, where Heidi's cousin Jenna was already waiting, looking at the list of cocktails.

"I didn't know they served these types of drinks here," she said, looking impressed.

"A new addition," Heidi told her. "But we've kept some old traditions, too."

Jenna's eyebrow shot up. "We?"

Uh-oh, Heidi felt the mood shift as the women all stared at her expectantly. "I mean, it's Ryan's bar. I was just the consultant."

"You made a good team." Maddie was fighting off a smile.

"And Cole too." Heidi seized the opportunity. "You'd barely know that the bar didn't always look this way. You'll have to check out the new lounge area. And isn't it so much

better with the pool table and dartboards moved out of sight?"

"Yes, but we weren't talking about Cole." Maddie took the signature drinks menu from Jenna and glanced at it. "So, did you two come up with this list together?"

"It was a joint effort, yes." Heidi tried to keep her tone professional, even though this night was very personal. And so was her connection with Ryan.

"Clearly you two work together very well." Maddie's eyes glimmered before she turned to put in her drink order.

"She's being ridiculous," Heidi said to Bella.

"Is she though? You can't deny that you guys succeeded in transforming this place. And I haven't heard any complaints about your living situation either."

"You sound like Candy," Heidi said, rolling her eyes.

"Or like someone who knows her sister," Bella said with a little smile. "And who's seen the way that man has been watching you from across the room."

Heidi's eyes widened as her cheeks heated and she elbowed her sister playfully. "Come on. Let's get a drink. It's a party and I've earned it."

She turned to the bar, fighting the urge to look over her shoulder. To see if what Bella had said was true. But she knew her sister, just as well as Bella knew her.

And she knew that there was no misunderstanding here at all. She was falling for Ryan. And maybe, he was falling for her too.

*

Jackson Bradford was the first to compliment Ryan on

the changes, after seeking him out near the bar, one of the new signature drinks in hand. Ryan and Heidi had worked on them all week, with Mitch's suggestions, and Ryan was paying attention to which ones were the most popular with the guests here tonight.

"If I'm not careful, you might just put the Carriage House out of business," Jackson said with an easy grin that showed there was no risk of that at all, or hard feelings.

Ryan and Jackson had gotten along when they were growing up, but they'd never been what most would call friends. Even though they were as different as the family establishments that they ran, Ryan also felt a kinship with Jackson, and a level of respect for how well he did what he did, pouring drinks, keeping the pub running effortlessly, always with a smile on his face, like he was enjoying every moment.

The truth was, though, that Ryan was smiling more lately, too. Harrison's was no longer a place of angst and a reminder of his shortcomings; it had become something he was feeling proud of, even excited about.

Mostly in part to Heidi, he thought, glancing across the room where she was deep in conversation with her sisters, matching peach-colored drinks in their hands called a "Sweet Sunset"; something that Heidi had promised him would be a hit with the ladies.

"I can't take all the credit," Ryan told Jackson. "Heidi's been consulting for me."

A knowing look passed through Jackson's face. He took a sip of his drink—this one a bourbon and orange concoction, served in a copper mug.

"Isn't that cozy."

"Please, I hardly have time to romance."

"And if you did?" Jackson looked intrigued, and Ryan was relieved that before he could respond to that unsettling question, Robbie came up and patted his brother on the back.

"What do you think? Can the Carriage House withstand the likes of this place?"

"Oh, I didn't change that much," Ryan said, feeling a little uneasy. He hadn't had a chance to speak with Kyle yet, but he'd seen the surprise on his brother's face when he'd come through the door. A lot of the installation had taken place after the table deliveries.

Now, his gut twisted at the thought that he'd taken things too far. Lost the soul of this place. The heart.

That with the shiny new fixtures and furniture, he'd stomped his father's mark right out of the pub he'd built from the ground up.

"I'm surprised you don't have a big reopening event planned," Jackson said, and Robbie nodded his agreement.

It had been considered, but ultimately Ryan felt that it would turn off the loyal patrons, the ones who had sat at this very bar and watched the transformation happen over the week.

"We're going to be offering some drink specials next Friday," Ryan said. He flicked his gaze over to Kyle, who was talking with Matt Bradford over in the lounge area.

"If you'll excuse me, I wanted to run something by my brother." He set his drink on the bar top and walked to the back of the room, where the fire was burning in the gas hearth, and the throw pillows Heidi had picked out had been pushed aside by the two men drinking beers.

"Have you tried one of our new signature cocktails?" Ryan asked, offering them each a menu.

He watched as Kyle skimmed it and then said, "I think I'll stick with a beer. I'm a simple guy."

He was. And he was also the kind of guy this place attracted. The guy who'd kept it afloat for years, and who had kept the old-timers happy, too.

"I'm game," Matt said. "Let me go see what Mitch has in mind."

Ryan stood alone with Kyle, knowing that the moment of truth had arrived. "So? What do you think? I can scale things back if you think I've gone too far with the transformation."

Even though he didn't want to. But he would. Because even though he was running this place, it wasn't just his. It was their family's.

"Are you kidding me?" Kyle looked at him in awe. "You've struck the perfect balance. You've done something I never could have envisioned, maybe because I didn't want to. I can't believe I'm saying this, but I think you love this place even more than I do, bro."

Ryan swallowed hard, realizing that might be true. Kyle had always been closer to their father. Ryan had tried to fit in, tried to stand out, and prove himself with good grades, getting into a good college, but he'd always felt like an outsider.

Now he realized the answer was in him all along. He just hadn't tapped into it before.

"Dad would be proud," Kyle said, reading his thoughts. "Actually, no. Dad would be impressed. Who knows, maybe little Brooke or Kyle Junior will end up taking it over someday. If you don't settle down soon and have kids of your own."

"You know how I feel about that." He rolled his eyes, even though he knew that Kyle was just messing with him.

"I know you've been hiding behind this place. But somewhere between hiding and sticking with it, this isn't the only thing that's changed. You have too, my brother."

"For the better, I hope?"

"Oh, most definitely." Kyle patted him on the shoulder. "So embrace it all. And stop hiding. You're out of excuses now."

Ryan pulled in a breath and, looking around at what Harrison's had become, let it out slowly. It was all he needed to hear. It had all been worth it.

And it was all thanks to the woman standing over near the three-tiered birthday cake, making a wish that he could only hope didn't include Lanie finding a new listing soon, so their time together would be over and done with for good.

*

"Oh, I'm tired." Heidi kicked off her shoes the moment she stepped into the house and didn't bother to set them in their proper place in the front closet. Instead, she scooped them up and carried them with her over to the couch, to be put in her bedroom later. She'd have no real reason to wear them again anytime soon—with their three-inch heels and painful back strap, they were probably best saved for a rare party, and one that did not involve dancing.

"Why do women wear shoes if they hurt?"

"Because they make my legs look nice," Heidi said, giving an ankle a little kick.

Ryan laughed, but his gaze fell to her legs and stayed there. Heidi's pulse sped up as she sat down.

"Too tired for a nightcap?" Ryan motioned to the bottle of champagne in his hand that he'd carried back from the pub, along with the leftover cake. "With all the excitement, I need to downshift a little before I try to sleep."

"You're probably right," Heidi agreed, pulling her bare legs under her on the sofa as she inched to the side, making room for him. "I'm pretty wound up, too. I'd say that tonight was a major success."

"And we have leftover cake for breakfast," Ryan said, returning from the kitchen with two wine glasses. Not exactly proper, and Heidi was surprised to see that he was loosening up.

"Cake for breakfast is the best part of a birthday," Heidi said. She scooted to the side of the couch to make room for him—but not too much room. His presence was obvious, warm, and comfortable, and she wasn't eager for the night to end anytime soon. "It goes along with cookies for breakfast at Christmas."

Ryan gave her a disapproving look and she swatted him away.

"How is it any different than a muffin?"

He nodded his head from one side to the next. "Has anyone ever told you that you have a great way of rationalizing your vices?"

"I'd like to think that I'm enjoying my life! If you can't eat cookies and cake for breakfast or ice cream out of the container, then you're missing out."

Ryan handed her a glass and clinked hers. "Happy Birthday. And thank you…for sharing it with me."

"Are you kidding? I couldn't believe the look on everyone's faces when they came in the door. And those signature drinks were a big hit, too. Didn't I tell you?" She beamed, but the intensity of Ryan's stare overwhelmed the teasing banter.

Ryan's gaze lingered on her for a moment. "I didn't just mean about Harrison's."

Oh. Heidi's heart began to race as she sipped her champagne, still chilled despite the warm walk home.

"Kyle seemed happy with the place," Heidi said, shifting gears.

Ryan nodded. "He was. He also said that Harrison's is on the path to success."

Heidi narrowed her eyes at him. "Why don't you sound more pleased about that?"

Ryan set his drink on the coffee table. "Because he made another point. He said I couldn't hide behind the bar anymore, which I realized is exactly what I've been doing ever since I came back to town. Without the weight of the business on me, I guess I have no more excuses."

"Going to be launching a social life, then?" Heidi couldn't help but wonder what that would look like. And if she'd be included in it.

"I see the way you're looking at me. I know what you think." He peered at her, but he was fighting off a smile.

"Couldn't I say the same for you? You're here at the house most days."

"Does that surprise you?" She assumed it would.

"In a way," he admitted. "I guess I'm surprised you're not out more with your clan, or…"

"My clan?" She laughed. But there was no denying she and her sisters and cousins—and their cousins—were a big, close family. She set down her glass and stretched out her legs. "They're all in relationships for the most part, and Natalie has Zoe."

"And you? You don't want to find someone?"

"I'll know when I find the right one," she said. "Isn't that how it usually works?"

He raised his eyebrows. "I thought I'd found the right one. Turns out I couldn't have been more wrong."

She winced, remembering what he'd told her. "Because she cheated?"

"Because…she was all wrong for me."

"And what does all right look like for you?" Heidi asked, only realizing just how suggestive that comment was when his gaze turned intense.

Her heart began to pound as the silence stretched and he looked at her, as if he was going to say something, confirm this emotion that had been growing in her all night, and even long before that. He was sitting close, their arms just an inch away from each other, their faces not much more. His eyes dropped to her mouth as he leaned in ever so slowly, and she didn't back up this time. Didn't want to.

Just as quickly, Ryan pulled back, cleared his throat, and stood. "I should get to bed. Early day tomorrow."

She blinked at him, thrown. A part of her wanted to ask what he was running from, but the other part of her didn't want to cast a shadow on what had otherwise been a very nice night. Unexpected, in every possible way.

"I'll...see you in the morning." Her own voice was hesitant because she didn't know what had just happened. A part of her was relieved that Ryan had sprung off the couch, but the awkwardness that lingered in the room only reminded her of how close she'd just felt to him and how much she longed to return to that moment.

Ryan had already moved to the kitchen and returned without his wineglass. "I'll probably get an early start, so don't worry about saving any of the cake for me." His smile seemed strained, like there was more he wanted to say.

Heidi held her breath, wondering if he would voice his thoughts, but instead, he just gave a little nod.

"Goodnight. And happy birthday, again."

Heidi waited until she heard the closing of his bedroom door before standing up and walking into the kitchen, where she swapped her champagne for the last pint of peanut butter ice cream in the freezer. She plucked a spoon from the door and pulled out a chair at the small table in the nook.

Something told her that she'd need all the help she could get if she was going to get any sleep tonight.

And maybe the same could be said for Ryan.

With her consulting work at Harrison's officially over, Heidi picked up more hours at the bookstore the next week, even though she was beginning to sense that her time here may be waning as well.

It wasn't even noon on Wednesday when she'd finished freshening up the window display, the front table, and the children's corner, which she'd turned into a rainy-day theme for the book Bella planned to read to them next. Not every day in summer was sunny, after all, and today was proof of that. She'd opened her eyes this morning to grey skies and steady showers…and a cup of delicious coffee waiting for her in the pot in the kitchen.

Ryan, however, had been keeping long hours all week, and she was beginning to take it a little personally.

"Well, this looks cute!" Bella grinned up at the colorful umbrellas that Heidi had popped open and hung from the light fixture that was centered over the bright yellow rug in this part of the shop.

"Seven years of bad luck for each umbrella, so you'd better think it's cute!" She folded the step ladder, admiring her own work.

"Or is that cracked mirrors?" Bella laughed. "You'd think I'd know all this working in a bookstore. I can go and look things like this up whenever I want."

"Or you could just pull out your phone and tap it into the internet search box," Heidi said as she stacked the last of the books for the kids and propped the top one slightly open.

"Oh, what fun would that be?" Bella gave her a frown. "Everything okay?"

Heidi thought quickly. There was no sense in telling her sister that she was feeling a little disappointed that she and Ryan seemed to have lost the connection that they were building. After all, unlike some of the other people in town, her sister had never insinuated that she hoped or expected more could blossom between the two of them. It would come as a big surprise to Bella to discover that Heidi didn't just tolerate Ryan, or that their relationship had extended beyond the renovation of Harrison's. Maybe there was something else there.

"Just feeling restless," she said, even though that wasn't a lie. The next part, however, was. "Rainy days make me stir crazy."

Bella, she knew, craved them. As a kid, she loved nothing more than curling up with a book or her notebook and disappearing into a fictional world for hours on end. Heidi used that time to get into mischief, as her family called it, often entertaining herself with potions from household products that weren't always best in combination, or painting a mural on her walls with nail polish, even if her mother never could bring herself to paint over it.

Well, until now. The family home was undergoing change, their childhoods were far behind them, but some things remained the same.

Heidi gave a little smile when she watched Bella pick up her novel and curl up into an armchair. George remained loyally at her feet.

"Mom was in here before the rain," Bella said, looking up.

Heidi groaned. "Please tell me that she's not still worried about my living situation?" Though she hadn't heard further on the subject from her mother, she knew that the topic was far from dropped.

"She just wanted to iron out the details for your birthday celebration. Your belated celebration, I should say." Bella raised an eyebrow. "She thinks you've been dodging her calls."

"Which would be true." Heidi knew she couldn't hide from her family forever, though. Nor did she want to. She just wanted to finally have some good news to share. "I've been really busy with Harrison's. This week is the first time I've had a chance to come up for air."

"That's what I told her," Bella said, but Heidi was far from relieved.

"Please tell me that she hasn't taken any encouragement from Candy in thinking that there could be something going on between me and Ryan."

"Why would Candy think that?" Bella said with such conviction that Heidi opened her mouth to explain before her sister couldn't hold back her laughter. "Don't worry, Mom just wants to make sure she knows when we can all come over for dinner, especially now that they're without a complete kitchen. I suggested we go to the Carriage House Inn one night instead if that's okay?"

A public setting would be more than okay. "Yes, you know my schedule, so go ahead and firm things up with Natalie."

"You don't have anything else in the works then? Now that your work at Harrison's is over?"

"Not yet." Heidi didn't make eye contact as she fussed around with some papers. Once again, she was standing in the way of her own success. Just a little differently this time.

Bella sighed and looked out the window. "It will be quiet all day until things dry up, and I'm not venturing out even if I am craving a rosemary scone."

George barked his displeasure before resuming his position. Heidi gave him a scratch behind the ears as she passed by with a stack of books. "Good thing you got him out for a few minutes then. It's really coming down now."

But the weather wasn't the only thing making her feel itchy and unsettled. There was the matter of Ryan, of course. The fire he'd lit in her now felt snuffed out, both personally and professionally.

While her sister enjoyed her lunch break reading a book, Heidi paced the space, looking for something to do, something that would inspire her. She couldn't leave the shop; she was on duty, even if she did feel like she shouldn't exactly be on the clock. But it went deeper than that, and panic built in her gut when she considered the many other times she'd felt this way. There was the job at the doctor's office, the one at the hair salon, the last time she had worked here, of course… Each time she'd felt this same sense of frustration. A nagging sense that she wasn't where she was supposed to be.

It was a feeling she didn't have last week. Or the week before. Working on Harrison's had been exciting, and so had seeing her ideas come to fruition, even success.

She glanced at the display window now, which was unabashedly better than it had been in the past, even though she knew Bella had tried and done a good enough job. But there were only so many tables to rearrange or window themes to create.

And this job was only part-time.

Chewing her lip, she walked past Bella to the counter. Her sister, like usual, looked up from her book. She missed nothing, and that was often just the problem.

"Okay, what's up?" Bella closed her book firmly, her steady eye contact indicating that she wasn't going to resume reading until she'd had her answer.

"I've been thinking more about what you said, about offering my services to other businesses."

A slow smile crept up Bella's face. "It's about time!"

Heidi felt her shoulders sag in relief. There was a part of her that still worried about letting Bella down. She had a track record of it, after all.

"I thought I might use this time to touch up my resume. If that's okay. Consider it my break, of course."

"It's more than okay! But I have one question. What made you have a change of heart?"

A change of heart. Heidi thought about the one person who managed to do just that…about her career, about her confidence, and even, about how she viewed him.

She shrugged her shoulders in response. "It snuck up on me."

*

The sound of pots clamoring in the kitchen was almost as obvious as the delicious smells wafting through the living room when Heidi arrived home later that day, her feet sore from so many hours standing, but her heart full of new possibilities and, maybe, newfound hope.

Slowly, she kicked off her shoes and toed them into the corner of the closet, padding barefoot into the kitchen where Ryan was crouched down, rummaging through the cabinets.

"Hey," she said, trying to sound casual, even as the words emerged strained.

She was relieved when he flashed her a grin and said, "I'm glad you're here."

"Oh?" Her heart sped up, wondering what he meant by that.

"Yeah, I'm grilling burgers and I can't seem to find the grill tongs. I thought I brought them with me."

Oh.

"I actually moved them," Heidi said. "They're over in the drawer closest to the back door."

The Ryan she thought she knew would have probably reprimanded her for touching his stuff, or explained his organization system to her until her lids drooped, but that wasn't Ryan at all, was it?

"A much better place for it," he said, finding the tool he was looking for.

Heidi glanced at the stove and saw a pan covered with a lid, resisting the urge to lift it and peek at what was inside.

The back door was open, and a cool breeze filtered through the screen, reminding her that the weather would eventually be turning, and that summer wouldn't last forever.

"You coming out?" Ryan said, opening the screen door.

"I think I'll change first," she said, buying some time.

She hurried out of the kitchen and down the hall to her bedroom, almost startled when she saw the perfectly made bed, and the desk free of clutter. She certainly hadn't lived like this before. Even at the carriage house, her dirty clothes were usually in a pile on the floor of her closet, and tugging the duvet up close to the pillows was about as close as she usually came to making the bed.

Maybe it was Ryan—not wanting to hear his disapproval, or maybe it was her. Either way, something had changed, and she liked it. Didn't want to go back to the way things were before.

Didn't really want to go back to living alone, either.

Maybe she'd get a pet when Ryan moved out. Or maybe…

Nonsense. This was a summer arrangement. But summer wasn't over yet.

Heidi changed into jeans and a tee shirt and then pulled her hair up into a ponytail. There was a stack of mail on the table nearest the door and she stopped to leaf through it, vowing that she wouldn't pay a single bill late ever again, not that Ryan would allow it, and he was splitting everything with her at the moment.

Her fingers settled on the creamy large envelope that was hidden below a furnishing catalog. She'd recognize Candy's elaborate scroll any day.

"I think we received Amelia and Matt's wedding

invitation," she said when she stepped outside onto the back deck. Unlike the front yard, which was small and confined, with a hedge of flowering shrubs that bordered the house and some finicky roses that lined the brick-papered path to the sidewalk, the backyard was lush with two trees, a fenced-in yard lined with perennials that Heidi was sure her mother would be able to name on sight, and a deck that housed a built-in bench on one side and a rather ancient grill in the corner.

Heidi took a seat at the faded wooden patio table and held up the heavy envelope.

Ryan turned his attention from the burgers for a moment and said, "We? Just one card?"

Sure enough, the address was personalized to them both. "Maybe they wanted to save money. These invitations can be very pricey." But the look in his eyes told her what she already knew. "Or maybe Candy is being…suggestive."

"That's a gentle word for it." Ryan laughed and flipped a burger. "So, what do you think we should do?"

Heidi sighed. She was tired just thinking of a conversation with Candy. "I'll talk to Amelia. I'm sure she'll give us another invitation. Or at least take a look at the seating chart. Not that I mind sitting next to you," she added quickly.

Ryan's back remained to her as he tended to the grill. The smell of the burgers wafted through the summer evening air, reminding Heidi of everything she loved about this time of year. The long days and cool breezes, afternoons spent swimming in the lake until her legs were so tired that she lounged on the hammock until the fireflies started filling the dusk, before she'd slip upstairs with the window near her bed open, letting in the smells and sounds of the season that would all too soon be replaced with snow.

"If we're going to be sitting together, then we don't really need to bother asking for a separate invitation. If they're so expensive," Ryan added, glancing over his shoulder.

Heidi lifted the envelope higher to hide her smile as she readjusted herself on the chair. "Unless you wanted to sit at the singles table?"

Ryan grunted out a sound and closed the lid of the grill. "Who wants to sit at the singles table?"

Heidi shrugged. No one that she knew, and definitely not her. Still, she couldn't speak for Ryan.

"People who want to meet other singles?"

"That scenario rarely works out. I should know. I was seated at one of the singles tables at Britt and Robbie's wedding."

He'd been seated at her singles table, actually, not that Heidi felt the need to mention this. She'd spent the evening chatting with Lanie and Natalie. Jackson had been at the head table, of course, as the brother of the groom. Ryan had eaten his food, made stilted conversation with the widow to his right who had flown in from Chicago where Britt used to work, and then eaten his cake in silence while everyone else mingled or hit the dance floor.

Heidi set down the invitation. "Well, if we're going to attend the wedding together then you can't sit there all night. You'd have to keep me company."

Ryan reached for his beer that he'd propped on the deck rail. "I could do that."

"You'd have to dance." Heidi lifted an eyebrow.

Sure enough, Ryan sputtered on his drink and began shaking his head firmly. "Yeah, sorry. I don't do that."

"Why not?" Heidi asked, genuinely interested. The man had a good body. A very good one, she thought, letting her gaze rest on his sculpted arms as he made a show of checking the burgers again, even though Heidi was pretty sure they could finish on their own at this point.

Ryan stalled by plating each one on a sesame bun. Heidi doused hers in ketchup when he disappeared into the kitchen, eventually returning with a plate of burger toppings and some seasoned potatoes—what she must have smelled when she'd walked in.

"You weren't joking about cooking," Heidi said after she'd topped her burger and taken a bite. "But for a minute there I thought you weren't coming back out."

Ryan slipped her a smile and took a bite of his food. "I was hoping you'd forget about the dancing stuff if I fed you a nice meal."

"Ah, but you were already planning on feeding me a nice meal even before I brought it up." Her chest warmed at the thought.

"As I said, it's easier to cook for two. I don't mind it; in fact, I sort of enjoy it. Beats takeout, even with the cleanup. But it feels pointless to go through the hassle just for myself."

"So, when Lanie finds you a new place to live in the fall, you'll be back to eating pizza or grub at the pub."

"Pretty much." The shadow on his face was replaced with a gleam in his eyes. "When she finds *you* a new place to live, that is."

"Nice try. And you haven't made me forget my question, either. Why are you so opposed to dancing?"

He thought about that for a moment. "I guess I never saw the point in it."

"And here I thought you were just afraid to let your guard down," Heidi joked, but this time Ryan didn't match her smile.

"That too, maybe." He stabbed a potato. "Some people say I take life a little too seriously." He rose his eyebrows at her and she knew she hadn't crossed a line. Yet.

Still, they were touching on something here, and she didn't want to press it. Didn't want to watch him clam up again or exit the room quickly like he had after the party. Didn't want to spoil this good feeling that was spreading through her like a warm summer breeze.

She got the sense that he didn't either.

"Look," she said, setting down her plate. "Everyone looks like a fool when they dance. It's part of the fun."

"See, that's the part I don't understand. How is that fun?"

"Maybe because once in a while it's nice to just jump around, listen to the music, zone out, and just respond to something other than life." Heidi picked a sesame seed off her burger. "It's joyful, don't you think? To live in the moment, share it with someone else, and not get bogged down about what others might think, or what's on your mind?"

"When you say it like that, I'm almost sold."

She twisted her lips into a smile and pulled her phone from her back pocket. "In that case, let me seal the deal."

She scrolled through her playlist until she found her favorite soundtrack, something not too slow, but not too fast either. She cranked up the volume and stood up, leaving her food half-eaten.

Ryan looked at her in obvious panic.

"What are you doing?"

"Teaching you how to dance." She held out a hand, but he shook his head. Setting the phone on the rail of the deck she reached out both hands, this time taking both of his in hers. He resisted, but not enough to show true protest, and her stomach rolled with something she couldn't describe at the sensation of his palms in hers. She waited for him to drop them once he'd somewhat reluctantly gotten to his feet, but instead, he dropped just one and wrapped the other around her waist.

Heidi blinked in surprise as he expertly swayed her to the music, even giving her a little twirl before pulling her close again.

She pulled her head back so she could look him in the eye. "You know how to do this!"

He gave a little smile. "Just because I know how to dance doesn't mean I like to."

"But…"

"My ex. She signed up for lessons once. And of course, I applied myself and made sure I learned all the moves, practiced in my free time and everything."

He was laughing at himself, and Heidi joined in, delighted.

"I learn something new about you every day."

"Something good I hope?" His smile reached his eyes before they dropped lower, down to her mouth. The music played, but they no longer moved to the beat, instead they stood, in each other's arms, her heart beating so fast that she was sure he could hear it hammering against his warm chest. His arm was firm on her back, low against her tailbone, and his mouth was so close, growing closer until there. It was warm, on her mouth, kissing her slowly, deeply, with the level of expertise that she'd only come to expect from him.

When he did something, he did it thoughtfully. Purposefully. And now she wondered just how long he'd been wanting to do just this.

Maybe as long as she'd been hoping he would.

"So I take it that we're going to the wedding together?" he said, giving her a slow smile when they broke apart.

"Now that I know you'll be dancing with me," she said, still a little breathless. And she wondered now if he intended to kiss her again too. "But that still doesn't explain why you sat out every dance at Britt's wedding."

"That's easy. There wasn't anyone I wanted to dance with."

Heidi faked an injured look even though she was a little hurt by his comment. "I was there, you know."

"I know." He gave a little smile. "But that night I was just enjoying watching you."

"Oh." She blinked, trying to process what he was saying. To rewrite the story she'd told herself.

Because she'd been very wrong about Ryan Harrison. And maybe, about herself, too.

13

The Firefly Café was as much a family business as the Conway Orchard and Winery, and the perfect place to host Brooke and Kyle's gender reveal party, even if Heidi suspected that Ryan might have liked to give Harrison's another chance at a celebration.

Candy, had, of course, outdone herself with the theme, from pigs in a blanket to pink and blue cocktails, to the chalkboard that usually listed the specials that now tallied everyone's guesses. Clusters of pink and blue balloons were gathered in every corner, and every table was covered in a white tablecloth and anchored with a pink and blue flower arrangement.

Heidi arrived with her sisters and her niece, not surprised to see her parents already standing at the back of the room, chatting with her Aunt Miriam and Uncle Steve.

"Team Blue or Pink?" Candy asked. It was clear which direction she was leaning from her pink ruffled top and matching nail polish, but then, Candy was never shy with her favorite color.

"Pink, of course!" Zoe said, then ran off to find Keira Bradford, snatching a pink cupcake along the way.

Natalie laughed as she watched her daughter. "Seems like just yesterday that was us."

"More like the two of you," Bella said, glancing at each of them. "I was always the quiet one."

"Nothing wrong with that," Heidi said, looking around for another quiet one and feeling disappointed that Ryan wasn't here yet. Still, he would show up, of course. He was the uncle to this baby, after all.

"I don't know about that," Bella said with a sigh. She studied the drinks that had been set up on the counter, lined with streamers and balloons. "Would it be wrong to drink a blue cocktail if I'm technically on Team Pink?"

"You and your rules!" Heidi shook her head fondly. "Are you afraid of getting in trouble with Candy?"

"Wouldn't you be?" Bella raised an eyebrow but, being the newfound rebel that she was, reached for a martini glass filled with an ocean blue liquid. "Oh, this is good. Worth it, even."

Heidi had been planning on playing by the rules today, but Bella swayed her. "Oh, why not? There will be plenty of champagne at Amelia's wedding next month, and every event leading up to it, too."

"Did you get your invitation?" Natalie sighed as she reached for a glass of champagne. "I don't have much hope for the singles table, but at least I have you to keep me company, Heidi."

Heidi averted eye contact by glancing at the door just in time to see Ryan step inside. He paused, momentarily stunned by the scene, which was quite over the top even for Candy, then caught her eye and slipped her a smile from across the room.

"Heidi?"

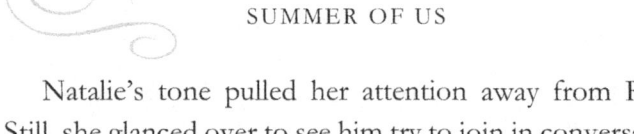

Natalie's tone pulled her attention away from Ryan. Still, she glanced over to see him try to join in conversation with the guys before Candy could swoop in on him. No such luck. She hid her smile behind her glass as she watched Candy commit him to a vote. Team Blue it was.

"Heidi?"

Heidi blinked and looked back at her sisters, who each stared at her with a knowing smirk.

"You're not going to be sitting at the singles table at Amelia's wedding, are you?" Bella said. A quick study, that one. Must have been all those books she read as a child.

Heidi decided that there was no point in denying it. The truth would come out sooner rather than later, especially when Candy was the one collecting the invitations.

"We only received one invitation to the house. So, it just made sense…"

Bella's eyes were large as she nodded her head slowly. "Oh, of course."

"It only makes sense." Natalie looked both mad and pleased. It was always a fine line with her. As the eldest, she felt she had a right to know these things, and advise accordingly. "But you and Ryan Harrison?"

Heidi felt her back stiffen. "What's so weird about that?"

"Well, you're just so…different," Natalie said.

"Ever heard the line that opposites attract?" Bella nudged her sister gently.

"Oh, says the bookshop owner who is happily dating an author." Natalie shook her head ruefully. "Where is Craig, by the way?"

"He's in Chicago this week. Cleaning out his old apartment. He's decided to make Blue Harbor his official residence."

There was no hiding how much this pleased Bella and Heidi was happy for her. Natalie, however, looked a little shaken. Of all of them, she'd dated the most, but was yet to find a second chance at love, if you could even call what she had with her ne'er do well first husband love at all.

"It'll happen for you," Bella said gently. "Look at Heidi. Who would have ever thought she'd find love this summer?"

"It isn't…love. It's just…" But Heidi didn't know how to describe it. Instead, she gave Natalie a smile of encouragement. "And Lanie will be at the singles table too, I'm sure."

"Gee thanks." Natalie took a long sip of her drink. "Another attractive woman to compete with."

"Speaking of Lanie, have you heard anything more about the fall market? She must know what's coming available soon." Bella was tactful, clearly picking up on Heidi's resistance to talking about Ryan too much, especially when he was in the room. And so was Candy.

But there was no doubt that come her next shift at the bookshop, she would be back on the hook.

Still, just thinking about the summer ending put an unsettling sensation in her stomach, and all at once, this happy moment seemed to come to a halt. "I haven't seen her around."

"You haven't called?" Natalie looked at her with alarm. "It's all fine and good to start dating Ryan, but living with

him? Take it from me, Heidi, you don't want to jump in without knowing how shallow the water is."

Heidi firmed her mouth against a mean comeback, knowing that her sister was speaking from a good place, and an honest one. Her husband had left her when Zoe was only two, never to be heard from again. Of course, she was cautious.

The implication, of course, was that Heidi wasn't. That she just floated through life, not thinking of the consequences. Maybe this had been her way, sure, but she wasn't that little girl anymore, even if they all seemed to think that she was.

"Don't worry, Natalie. I'm a big girl. I can take care of myself." She gave her sister a smile she didn't quite feel and saw an opportunity to exit the conversation when Gabby and Jenna came in through the door. No doubt the cousins would serve as a good distraction from her sister for a while. By the time the carefully frosted cake was cut, the only topic of conversation would be the new baby, and suggestions for names, of course.

As Heidi ducked past Candy with her head low, she heard the woman remarking to Gabby that she already had a list of girl names selected. Heidi was still chuckling when she moved out onto the enclosed porch at the back of the café, admiring the sweeping lake views nearly as much as the buffet table where Maddie was guarding the gorgeous cake with white buttercream frosting in intricate balloons and teddy bears dancing around it.

"It's too pretty to cut!" Heidi remarked.

"Wouldn't stop Candy from poking her finger in it,"

Maddie said with a pinch of her mouth. She narrowed a glance in Candy's direction.

"Is that what you're doing?" Heidi laughed and popped a mini quiche into her mouth. The theme, of course, was mini. Everything was small. What could be colored pink or blue had been, right down to the bite-size blueberry and raspberry tarts.

"Would you trust her?" Maddie remarked. "But I'm dying for a glass of that champagne and a quick trip to the ladies' room."

"Let me guard your post," Heidi offered.

"Watch it carefully," Maddie said, resting a hand on her arm. She darted another peek at Candy, who, caught staring directly at the cake, fluffed her blond curls and looks away with such dramatic nonchalance that even Maddie had to laugh.

Not too worried about Candy, Heidi grazed on the buffet, hovering close enough to her post and waiting for Maddie to return. The conversation in the room was lively, and the space was crowded with the Conways, the Conway cousins, and the Clarks. Brooke's branch of the Conway family bridged the two other families, and for as long as Heidi could remember, they had all united as one, gathering for every wedding, holiday, and now, baby shower.

"The bigger question than whether it will be a girl or a boy is whose turn will it be next?" She heard one of the men say.

Heidi sipped her drink and took a step back, eager to hear the response. Her bet was on Robbie Bradford. She knew from firsthand experience that Keira was longing for

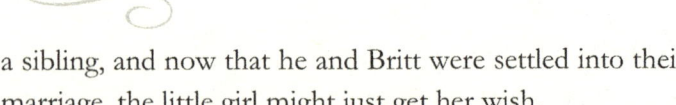

a sibling, and now that he and Britt were settled into their marriage, the little girl might just get her wish.

"Robbie for sure," a voice—Matt—said.

Heidi gave a knowing smile. No surprise there.

"But Jackson, you'd better get on it, old man. You too, Ryan," Robbie teased.

Heidi's heart began to drum and she edged closer to the open window that divided the sunroom space of the restaurant from the main dining room.

"You're playing house with Heidi Clark," Jackson said. "You're one step ahead of me."

"That's only temporary," came Ryan's voice. "And it certainly wasn't planned."

Heidi's heart seemed to stall in her chest, and she realized that her hand had started to shake. Nothing going on? But that kiss—that kiss wasn't nothing. That kiss was intentional. Everything that Ryan did was thought out, planned even.

Except, that wasn't true, was it? She'd seen that he was willing to be spontaneous, throw caution, and live in the moment.

And maybe, that's exactly what he'd done. While she...she'd done the opposite.

Opposites attract. Her sister's words haunted her. As did her other sister's warning.

"She's always been pretty," Kyle said, but this did little to boost Heidi's spirits. There was only one opinion that mattered right now, and she was holding her breath, waiting for the words that would tell her everything she needed to know.

"We all know what Heidi's like," Ryan said.

Heidi felt her mouth go dry. Yes, them and half the town.

"If there's one thing I've learned from relationships, it's that I'm better off alone than with the wrong person," Ryan said.

"Ryan probably has a spreadsheet with all the traits he's looking for," Kyle said with a laugh.

Probably, Heidi thought, blinking back tears. And no doubt she didn't check any of the boxes.

She managed a bright smile when Maddie reappeared on the sun porch, casting one more warning glance over her shoulder as Candy tried to stop her, pleading for a hint.

"She won't let up until that cake is cut. I'm the only one who knows the gender, and I've been sworn to secrecy!" Maddie tsked and then popped a tart into her mouth. She gave Heidi a funny look. "Everything okay?" Her eyes darted to the cake, which she now inspected carefully. "Candy didn't try to swipe off the frosting, did she?"

"What? No." Heidi blinked, slow to the uptake. "No, I just...I'm not feeling well. Must be this blue cocktail. Who knows what goes into it to make it blue."

Satisfied that Candy hadn't poked any holes in the surprise, Maddie relaxed her shoulders and smiled. "I could tell you, but I think you'd better get some more air instead. You look a little flushed."

"It's warm in here. I'm sure that's it." Heidi was grateful for the excuse to leave. "I think I'll just take a quick walk, down by the lake."

"Don't miss the reveal!" Maddie called after her, and Heidi knew that she couldn't.

She'd have to face Ryan one more time. But that would be the last time.

*

It was a girl. Possibly, no one was more thrilled than Candy, who cheered and screamed so loud, that Brooke's mother was rendered speechless.

"You'd think Candy was going to be the grandmother," Bella said, laughing as they walked up the gravel path toward Main Street. She glanced at Heidi when they reached the corner. "You've been awfully quiet. Are you okay?"

"Why wouldn't I be okay?" Heidi asked, but her chest still ached as the words echoed in her mind. She was barely listening to Bella.

"Oh, I don't know, because you're walking home with me instead of Ryan?"

"Please." Heidi scoffed. "Haven't you always known me to be an independent person? I don't need a man to make me happy."

Her voice caught on that last line, but luckily Bella didn't seem to notice. "No, you never did. Neither did I. But there's something to be said for finding a great guy, isn't there?"

Heidi wasn't sure how much longer she could pretend like nothing was wrong, but she was too exhausted tonight to get into anything. Instead, she thought of the problems that loomed, and how to best deal with them.

"I actually got a call from Lanie while we are at the party. A new listing came up and I...I think I'll take it. I might just need to stay with you a bit if your offer still stands?"

Bella was looking at her strangely now. "Of course, you're always welcome with me and George, if you don't mind all his dog hair on the couch." She tipped her head. "Are you sure everything is okay? Natalie upset you today, didn't she?"

Someone had upset her, all right, but it wasn't Natalie. What Natalie had said had been brutally true, and Heidi would have benefited from hearing her words—and heeding them—long before today.

"I think she made a good point, actually. This living arrangement isn't working out. It never was. It was supposed to be my place—or his. Not both of ours. It wasn't supposed to be the summer of us…sharing something. It was a big mistake." In oh so many ways.

"Okay, well, when do you want to come stay?"

"Tonight?" Heidi knew she was pressing things, maybe even imposing, but wasn't that what she'd always done? Looked to her family to help her or bail her out? What was one more time?

Because this time, she vowed, it would be the last. Gone were the mistakes in her career. And now, gone were the mistakes with her heart.

"I mean, why wait, right?" Heidi said.

She could tell by the look in Bella's eyes that there would be some explaining to do, and she would, but first, she needed to get into that cottage, pack up her stuff, and get out.

Preferably before Ryan even knew she was gone.

*

Ryan stopped by Harrison's on the way home from the party, pausing on the street to view it from a distance, the way a tourist might, or someone who hadn't bothered to look through the window in a long time. Someone who had judged it, mistakenly so, perhaps, and written it off.

Inside, the room seemed to glow with warm light from the candles on the tables and the rustic light fixtures that replaced the more modern ones he'd first attempted. Mitch was tending bad, and Ryan grinned when he saw him shake a martini before pouring it into a glass and sliding it to a smiling patron. Lenny and Walter's personalized barstools were empty even though some people had to stand at the bar because there were so many people inside.

People were engaged, laughing, and even sharing plates off the new menu.

It was like looking into a part of him that had been untapped all this time. And there was just one person he wished could be standing beside him, seeing it all.

His father, he knew, could already see it. Had been there every step of the way. Maybe had even played a hand in positioning things in a helping manner. Nudging a certain person into his life.

Ryan grinned and quickened his pace down the street. The cottage wasn't far now, and he held up a hand in a wave when he saw Heidi coming out of the front door. His arm fell when he saw she was carrying two duffel bags and dragging a suitcase in each hand.

"What's going on?" he asked as he approached. "Are you going on a trip?"

Heidi didn't meet his eye as she adjusted the bag on her

shoulder. It was awkward and he reached out to help, but she turned her back to him just enough to make him realize that something was wrong.

"I'm moving out, actually."

He could only stare at her as he tried to make sense of what could have transpired since the party ended.

"Lanie found a great new place for me. It's probably more my style anyway, and you really like this place, so…" Her hair fell in a curtain, hiding her face. He resisted the urge to reach out, tuck it behind her ears, and force her to look at him.

"So you're moving out, just like that?" He stood, planted on the sidewalk, refusing to budge until he'd heard the truth.

Heidi sighed and finally looked at him for a brief, fleeting moment. Her eyes were shiny, her smile too bright. "All good things must come to end eventually, right?"

"Heidi." He frowned, trying to understand what was happening here, why she'd make such a sudden change.

"It's getting dark," she said, pulling in a breath. "I'll slide the key under the door one day this week when I come back for the rest of my stuff."

"Heidi." He stepped out in front of her to block her, but she took a step back.

"It was only temporary," she told him firmly. "It was only for the summer."

"But summer's not over yet," he told her.

The set of her eyes spoke more than her words. "It is for us."

14

Heidi was roused the next morning by a wet nose and a warm lick on her cheek. She opened one eye to see George looking back at her with hopeful eyes and an eager smile.

There were certainly worse ways to start her day, even if the heartache did settle in as soon as she sat up. Gratefully, she accepted the mug of coffee that her sister was extending to her. Bella was already dressed, and Heidi was relieved that it was her day off from the shop, even if she could have used a distraction right about now.

"This is good coffee," she said, taking another sip. She stiffened when George leaped onto the couch, nearly sloshing the mug, but Bella just regarded her puppy with fondness. "You're spoiling him, you know."

"I used to spoil you, too," Bella said ruefully. She dropped onto the armchair and took a sip of her own coffee. "You were just so cute and playful. It was hard not to give in to you, especially when you had those pigtails."

Heidi smiled back on those days. "Natalie was always styling my hair. I suppose I was good practice for Zoe."

Bella gave her a sad smile. "I think a part of us will always see you as that bright-eyed little girl with the contagious spirit. But we're nearly the same age and certainly at the same stage in life. It's not really fair of us. I'm sorry."

Heidi stared at her sister. For so long she had yearned to hear those words, but now they felt like they were coming out of nowhere. "Where is this coming from?"

"It's long overdue. At work, I know we both try to keep our sisterly relationship out of the business side of things." They exchanged a look. Their professional differences had come between them before and they had both made a choice to do better this time. "But look at you, Heidi. You've turned my store around. You've turned Harrison's around, too. You host a better dinner party than most people in town, too. Well, maybe with the exception of Amelia."

Heidi managed a smile. "Ryan helped. He also gave me the opportunity at Harrison's."

"And he didn't have to. And you didn't have to make such a big success of it, either. So...are you finally going to tell me what's going on with the two of you?"

"Nothing," Heidi said flatly.

It took only a moment for Bella to read her tone. Her sister was more of a reader of people than books sometimes.

"What do you mean, nothing? Did something happen?"

Heidi sighed and stared down at the mug in her lap. George had curled up into a ball on her blankets by now and she stroked his silky fur, already feeling more at peace. Honestly! Who needed a man when you could have a dog?

That would be her next big step. Once she found a place to live, that was.

Panic quickened her pulse when she considered that she'd implied to Bella she would only be staying the week.

Maybe Craig could stay here and she could take his place for a while? August was closing in on them. For sure something would open soon.

She checked the clock on the wall. Too early to call Lanie.

"I don't think it's going to work out with Ryan," she said, feeling the tightness in her chest of disappointment. "It's like you said, we're too different."

"I was just surprised is all. And just yesterday you were positively blushing at his name. I assumed I should call Mom today to let her know we'll be adding another person to our reservation tonight."

Heidi groaned into her coffee. "I forgot about tonight. Would it be wrong to say I can't make it?"

"To your own birthday dinner?" Bella stared at her. "Okay, now I know something is going on. Explains why you're on my couch too. Did something happen at the party?"

Heidi could still hear the words in her ears, as clear as if Ryan were standing behind her now.

"What we had was just...temporary. All of it. The living arrangement, the work at Harrison's, and...whatever it was that was evolving between us."

Bella looked at her carefully. "You're sure?"

She should be sure, but there was a part of her, maybe that part of her that Natalie recognized and had tried to rein in, that dared to think that there was hope.

But where had these carefree thoughts ever gotten her before? She was thirty years old. It was time to face reality once and for all.

"Because I'd hate for you to walk away from something too soon, without giving it a fair chance."

Her old defenses prickled. Heidi sat up straighter and lifted her chin. "And what's that supposed to mean? That I'm a quitter?"

"No." Bella sighed, seeming exasperated. "I mean...I might have thought that before." She grimaced and set her mug down on a coaster. "But I don't mean that now, Heidi. I mean what I said. You're an accomplished woman. You have a lot of successes behind you and a lot more ahead of you. I guess I'm just trying to figure out why Ryan isn't worth fighting for? Usually, when you put your mind to something you feel strongly about, you don't give up. The opposite of quitting."

Heidi managed a slow smile. She knew what Bella was referencing. She had to wear her sister down to open her mind and change some things in the store, and she'd done it because she cared. About her sister. And her ideas.

And she cared about Ryan, too. Much as she wished she didn't.

"You know yourself the best," Bella said, checking her watch and standing. She paused to give Heidi one last look. "But I know you, too. When something doesn't work for you, you have no trouble walking away. But when something matters, you see it through."

And which was it? Heidi thought.

George lifted his head and turned back to look at her with big brown eyes before snuggling deeper into the blankets.

"My sentiments exactly, George," Heidi said.

*

Harrison's was slow, not that Ryan was too concerned. It was a Sunday afternoon and most people were outside, sitting by the lake, or strolling down Main Street. The Bloody Mary bar had been a hit this morning, though, and he made a note to place an order for more supplies before the day was out.

For the first time in a year, the fate of Harrison's wasn't weighing on his mind. Something else was. Or rather, someone else.

He looked up to see Kyle striding across the floors, admiring the tables, his own contribution to the space.

"Looks good, doesn't it?"

Kyle nodded, looking around the room. "Crowd looks good, too."

Ryan glanced from the corner of the bar, where Lenny and Walter sat in their designated chairs, feeling quite special, even they did grumble their gratitude. The rest of the bar was filled with faces that Ryan didn't recognize, younger guys, a few couples, tourists, most likely, enjoying some of the new menu items.

"So why don't you look happy?" Kyle slid into a barstool at the opposite end of where the old-timers sat. "Only one thing can make a guy who should be happy look so beaten down."

"Heidi moved out," Ryan said, sticking to the facts. Really, that could be all it was, but he knew it wasn't true. Even if Lanie had found her another place, which seemed unlikely but not impossible, there was a coldness in Heidi's eyes and tone that hadn't been there in all the time they'd spent together.

Hadn't ever been there in all the times he could remember. Heidi was bubbly and bright and she let troubles roll off her in a way that once alarmed him and now made him admire her.

"I assume there's more to it than that." Kyle spread his hands on the bar. He'd always said he loved the feel of the wood under his palms. "I assume there's more to you and Heidi than just a shared cottage, too."

"Maybe there was." Ryan shrugged. "Not anymore. Whatever there was is over."

"You sure?" Kyle squinted at him. "A while back I could have said the same thing about me and Brooke, and look at us now."

"That's different. You and Brooke are married. You had a reason to work it out. Heidi and I barely know each other." Except that wasn't true. He'd gotten to know Heidi over these past few weeks. Gotten to really understand her. And maybe, fall in love with her.

"Besides, what happened between you and Brooke was my fault."

Kyle looked at him sharply. "That's not true. My separation from Brooke was my fault, really. Brooke even sometimes considers it to be her fault."

Ryan wasn't accepting that. "If I'd taken over the bar, or stepped in and done my duty, you could have moved to New York with Brooke as planned."

"And I chose to stay, instead of go. And Brooke chose to go. This is on us, Ryan. Please don't tell me you've been blaming yourself for my relationship problems." When Ryan didn't immediately reply, Kyle shook his head. "The

past is behind us. We both made our choices in the moment. You had a job and a relationship in Cleveland."

"A relationship that didn't work out," Ryan reminded him.

"Is that what this is about?"

Ryan couldn't be sure. "I held on to a job and a relationship that wasn't right for me in the end, probably longer than I should have because to admit that they weren't working out when you'd given up so much to run this place…" He shook his head, but Kyle just blew out a breath and leaned back in his chair.

"Wow. Okay, stop right there. I made my choice and looking back, I probably would have made the same one. I love this place. Love and resent it sometimes, sure, but it's a part of our family, and if it came down to letting it close or giving up a few years of my life, I'd do it all over again."

"Me too," Ryan said, thinking back on the past year. "I want this place to keep going."

"And it will. Partly in thanks to Heidi."

Ryan shook his head. "I have a bad track record with women."

"Not every relationship is doomed to failure," Kyle said.

"And not every relationship is made to succeed," Ryan countered.

Kyle looked a little sad. "That's not the big brother I know. You were always the one who saw things through. What could work, did work. You just have to recognize the difference."

Ryan was quiet for a moment. Deep down he knew that

there were problems in his old relationship, that he was holding onto something that wasn't there, probably longer than he should.

He'd never stopped to think that maybe the reason he'd done it was because he was afraid to admit he'd failed at something.

"Look at this place. You could have walked away."

"You could have too," Ryan said. "But this is our family history. All we have left of Dad."

"I just ran it. You turned it around. Deep down I think you knew you could or you wouldn't have taken it over from me. You would have found something better to spend your time on, even here in Blue Harbor."

Ryan raised his eyebrows. It was possible, even if he didn't like to think about it. He shook his head. "Business and relationships are two different things."

"True, but what does your gut say?" Kyle asked. "Because you know that half the time it's right. You had a feeling about this place. It was your time for it." Kyle grinned and opened his arms wide to the empty room.

Ryan couldn't fight the swell of pride.

"The question is whether the time is right for something else, too. Or should I say, someone?" Kyle stood up. "It's Sunday night. You coming for dinner?"

That pulled a smile from him. "I'd never miss a Sunday dinner."

"Unless there's somewhere else you need to be today. Just keep me posted." Kyle grinned over his shoulder and pushed out the door.

Ryan was still shaking his head long after Kyle had left,

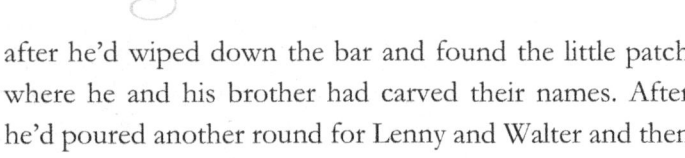

after he'd wiped down the bar and found the little patch where he and his brother had carved their names. After he'd poured another round for Lenny and Walter and then handed off their tab to Mitch.

He stopped on his way out to run his finger over the etching on the bar once more, grinning slowly. Kyle was right about him knowing deep down that he could make something of this place, once he figured out how.

And he was right about knowing something else in his gut, too. Heidi might not be his best match on paper, and she might not be the person he'd thought he'd been looking for. But she was everything he'd been searching for and had finally found, and his heart knew that, more than his head.

Leave it to his kid brother to go and know more than him.

*

The Carriage House Inn was a comfortable spot for the Clark family because the owners—the Bradfords—were like family themselves. And no matter how heavy her heart might be, Heidi couldn't help but grin when she saw Jackson carrying over a complimentary bottle of champagne, especially for the occasion.

"It's a belated birthday," she told him after he'd popped the cork.

"It's still a birthday, and an important one, too." He filled their glasses, skipping Zoe, who had been treated to a kiddie cocktail instead, and then left them to decide on the menu, even though they all knew all the offerings.

"With Craig away this week, it's like the old days," their mother said, admiring all of her daughters across the table.

Yep, just like the old days, and a glance from Natalie confirmed what was on Heidi's mind. They were now all in their thirties, officially. And still single, still celebrating with their parents, their childhood family. Plus Zoe, of course.

It was special, and Heidi wouldn't trade it for the world, but it also made her once again question her future, and what it might hold, professionally and personally.

"What's everyone going to order?" her father asked, opting for his beer rather than the flute of fizzing champagne.

"The usual," they all said, then laughed.

Heidi's smile faded, and she glanced over her shoulder to the bar, hoping to get Jackson's attention, but her heart sped up when she saw whom he was talking to.

She turned back to the table, where her family sat unaware of her dry mouth and racing pulse, listening to Zoe talk about a new art project she was making at camp.

Heidi glanced around the room, toward the door, wondering if she could dash out before Ryan saw her. If he hadn't already seen her.

Maybe, she thought, he had seen her. And he'd leave without saying anything.

It would be more than she could bear.

"I'll be right back," she said, pushing back her chair.

Only Bella seemed to pick up on anything amiss as she caught Heidi's eyes. Always a quick one, she glanced around the room, her mouth pinching when she looked in the direction of the bar.

Heidi knew that she could hide in the bathroom until he'd gone, that, of course, this was where her family was expecting her to go, but they were deep in conversation now, only Bella distracted by the turn of events, and Heidi marched purposefully toward the door, her plan stopping in its tracks when she hit the lobby.

She could run up the stairs to the rooms of the inn, even though she had no business being up there. Or maybe she could duck outside, stand around the corner, and text Bella who was no doubt scoping out the pub.

She had only made it halfway across the lobby when she heard her name. Closing her eyes, she stopped, wondering if she should bother to turn. There was nothing he could say to her that he hadn't already said. Nothing that could undo his true feelings. Or her reputation.

"Heidi, please wait. I've been looking all over town for you."

That had her attention. Suspicious, she turned, hating the way the sight of his khaki shorts and preppy polo made her stomach tighten a little, when once she might have rolled her eyes at his uptight ways.

"Yes?" She folded her arms over her chest. She'd be darned if she graced the man with a smile. He probably wanted to know what her plans were for removing her things, when she'd be stopping by, dropping off the key.

He hesitated for a minute as if he had changed his mind about what he planned to say. "A customer was in at the bar today. First time in years. She's opening a new place in Pine Falls. She was full of praise for the transformation."

Heidi pinched her mouth. "That must have made you feel proud."

"It should make you feel proud, too." His eyes softened with uncertainty she wasn't used to seeing. "I told her who was really responsible for the vision. She wants to meet you. She wants your input on her new place."

Heidi's pulse skipped and she knew she couldn't keep the surprise out of her expression. "It wasn't all my doing, though."

"I just wrote the checks," Ryan corrected her. "You turned the place around, Heidi. You turned my life around."

Heidi backed up, shaking her head. She didn't need him to soften the blow, to try to make nice because he felt like a jerk. Because he'd realized he'd been ungrateful, or even mean.

She didn't know what she needed him to do. Leave maybe. Walk away. Only somehow, standing here now, still sensing a bond between them, she wasn't sure she wanted that, either.

"I missed you last night," he said, silencing all those thoughts. "I mean, now that you've moved out, or are moving out, the house feels pretty empty."

"I'd think you'd like having a quiet place without all my loud energy," she said, unable to keep the bitter edge from her tone. When he frowned, she said, "I know what you think of me, Ryan. I heard what you said when you were talking with the guys yesterday at the café."

Ryan frowned, his eyes shifting as if searching for something he couldn't quite find. "What did I say?"

Heidi tipped her head. "Come on, Ryan. I heard you. Do I really need to repeat your hurtful words? Your true

assessment of me? I get it, okay, a lot of people think that way of me. I'm overly casual, I'm uncommitted, and I float through life. That I'm loud and overly talkative and wild." She held up a hand. "Believe me, I've heard it all."

"But you didn't hear it all," Ryan said. He stopped walking, forcing her to do the same. "You didn't hear the rest of what I said."

She hesitated, unsure if she was willing to hear him out, but the pleading look in his eyes made her stop.

"Okay, then, what did I miss?" She folded her arms over her chest, waiting for it.

"You're all those things. And then some," he said, giving her a small smile that she didn't match. "And that's why…that's why I like you."

She swallowed hard. She hadn't been expecting that. "Oh."

"And I was sort of hoping that you liked me too. Even though I'm old and boring, and what's that word you like to use? Uptight?"

"You can be a little uptight," she said, fighting off a smile.

"Maybe that's why we're a good team."

She shook her head. "We're more than a team. We're…good for each other."

"We are," he agreed, giving her a slow grin.

"Guess we have the Tinleys to thank for that," she said. "And Lanie. Showing us that awful apartment."

They shared a grin. "I know how much you like the cottage. If you want to stay, I can take the other place Lanie found."

Heidi brought her hand to her mouth to cover her laugh. "The other place is my sister's couch."

He didn't look surprised, but he did look pleased. "You mean?"

"There's no other place for me but that cottage. And there's no one I'd rather be sharing it with you."

Ryan pushed out a sigh and stepped closer to her, taking her hand. "Come on, then. Let's go home."

"I can't," she said, a smile curving her mouth when she saw the disappointment in his eyes. She took his hand and squeezed it. "I have a family dinner to get back to first. You coming?"

He grinned. "I wouldn't miss it."

"There's one thing you have to do first," she said, giving him a sly smile. "Kiss me."

"Like I needed to be asked," he said, wrapping his arms around her.

ABOUT THE AUTHOR

Olivia Miles is a *USA Today* bestselling author of feel-good women's fiction with a romantic twist. She has frequently been ranked as an Amazon Top 100 author, and her books have appeared on several bestseller lists, including Amazon charts, BookScan, and USA Today. Treasured by readers across the globe, Olivia's heartwarming stories have been translated into German, French, and Hungarian, with editions in Australia in the United Kingdom.

Olivia lives on the shore of Lake Michigan with her family.

Visit www.OliviaMilesBooks.com for more.

Made in United States
North Haven, CT
27 July 2024

55491948R00136